MW01596499

Four for Texas

A Quartet of Short Stories set in the Lone Star State

Flo Fitzpatrick

Treasures: A Mystery

Labor Day/Ladies Night: An Unusual Romance

Wilkinson Roses: A Ghost Fairy Tale

Center Floor: A Memoir

Cover photo *Texas Sunset* by Barb Woodward

© 2015

TREASURES

An iron fence surrounded the State Home on three sides. To the east were the once-elegant homes of the late 19th Century. By 1965, they were nothing more than grim shells, unsuccessfully attempting to hide the poverty within. The west side bordered busy 18th Street, with its eclectic mix of auto repair shops, Tex-Mex cafes and barbeque restaurants, pool halls disguised as family diners, and five-and-dime general stores that lured pre-teens inside and off the hot sidewalks with their aisles tempting the promise of beauty through cosmetics, and the dream of movie magazines. A small clearing south of the fence led visitors past neat grounds and solid dormitories. Behind the State Home to the north was a hodge-podge of shrubs, trees, weeds and what might best be classified as a dirt road leading nowhere. A huge *No Trespassing* sign, tacked to a small portion of fencing, rendered this wilderness forbidden, and therefore enticing to adolescents with a taste for adventure.

My best friend, Jean Rose Callahan, had been a resident of the Home since 1955, when her parents died in an accident. She shared a suite and a bath with three other girls in the dormitory closest to the creepy road. Her bed and dresser stood near a large window. Due to her seniority among her roommates, she'd been gifted with a little extra space, so she'd placed a screen around her cubbyhole for privacy. Photos of her parents, taken by a professional photographer in some other town, had been framed, and then placed next to the one I'd snapped with my Brownie camera, showing Jean holding my dog, Lugnut, in her arms, as she stood next to my Dad's old Buick Skylark convertible. The only other object on her dresser was an antique jewelry box. It had belonged to Jean's grandmother, and Jean once told me it was her lifeline to sanity. I understood. The bracelets and pendants were all she had of family. The kids at the Home had little space and less money, so they didn't own a lot of what my mom called 'dust collectors.' Jean spent a lot of time at her window, gazing at the tall trees and thorny shrubbery behind the great fence.

I was lucky. I had a great home, complete with parents and five older brothers, but I hung out as often as possible at Jean's. The State Home was no bed and breakfast, but my siblings couldn't come trotting by on an hourly basis, and Jean and I didn't have to contend with five daily different arguments about who had control of the record player or the television. I could make the six miles from my house to the Home on my semi-brakeless bicycle with little effort, and in the summer, did so every day.

Jean and I would spend hours experimenting with make-up after studying the photos in our favorite movie magazines. My pale skin, blonde hair and blue eyes worked better with the pastel pink lipsticks and cobalt blue eyes shadows offered by Mary Quant. Jean's dark, olive skin, inherited from a Lebanese mother and curly brown hair courtesy of an Irish dad never lent themselves to the whole British fashion look, so she created a style very much her own. Both of us loved the long, straight hair made popular by English models and actresses, but Jean's always waved even after ironing, so she'd cut hers super short the summer of '65, giving her the appearance of an Arabian leprechaun.

If we weren't painting our faces, we were listening to the Beatles while discussing boys and our future lives—both preferably in England. Jean wanted to be a reporter and break the hearts of famous men as she traveled the world. At fourteen that sounded extremely glamorous. I wanted to be an actress or marry Paul McCartney. At fourteen, I'm not sure which was most important, but I was taking drama in school in case the McCartney wedding never materialized. If we got bored with all the girly stuff we'd head across 18th Street to roam through The Shopping Center, which was nameless in 1965 and stayed nameless until it was finally torn down by a franchise fast-food drive-through many years later. The small strip mall consisted of one five-and-dime, a wallpaper, paint, and hardware shop, two beauty parlors, a barber shop, and the pièce de résistance simply known as *Wanda's*.

Wanda's was a bar and grill that prided itself on its status as a clichéd Texas diner, did a voluminous business and was our favorite place to camp for hours during afternoons that grew too hot to venture outdoors.

There was no Wanda. We were never sure whether there'd *ever* been a Wanda. The establishment was owned and operated by Gerald Hampton Johnstone, an ex-Marine who'd served in World War Two. Mr. Johnstone proudly displayed a Semper Fi tattoo on his right arm and always had a Navy Cross medal pinned to his left shirt pocket. Each day he hoisted the American flag up a pole in front of the diner following a short morning ceremony, and kept it there until sunset. He loved kids, dogs, the Lone Star state, Lone Star beer, and his own cooking. With the impudence of young teens, Jean and I would debate whether his nickname, Hamp, came from Hampton or Mr. Johnstone's unfortunate resemblance to a laundry hamper; i.e. short, squat, with a wide mouth. We adored him.

Wanda's served beer to customers of age, iced tea with free refills to teetotalers and teens, and fresh milk to children. *Wanda's Special* was the same every day. Chicken-fried steak with cream gravy, baked potato, salad and a basket of rolls. The salad was served in a side bowl the size of an ice-cream scoop, and consisted of lettuce, one tomato, and one jalapeno pepper. Choice of dressing could be found on each table in large plastic, squeeze bottles. Thousand Island or Ranch. Period. The gravy was also provided on the side in a bowl bigger than the salad itself, the potatoes were mutant giants swimming in butter (sour cream on the side) and the rolls were homemade sourdough.

Wanda's Special was a treat for the palate and the pocketbook at only $1.39. For an extra nickel, one could order coconut cream pie with real whipped cream.

Jukeboxes took up a good fifty-percent of each table. The other fifty-percent of *Wanda's* actual space was taken up with pool and Ping Pong tables in the rear of the diner. Older guys from the State Home would hang out by the game tables. Jean and I would hang out by the guys. They couldn't date us. After all, at fourteen we were still considered babies, and the lofty sixteen and seventeen-year olds looked on us as cute little sisters, who were occasionally bothersome, but they liked showing off their prowess at pool or table tennis and we were always an appreciative audience.

We learned the finer points of pool from Danny, the blonde, hazel-eyed captain of the track team at Lakeside High who hustled unsuspecting customers who happened to be up for a game. Mike showed us how to pick locks, a skill I firmly believe should be taught to all kids once they hit age eleven. I had a secret crush on Mike, the only boy who could ever beat me at Ping Pong. He was about six-two, and dark-haired with insanely long lashes and sapphire blue eyes. Jean had a thing for Rudy, the offensive tackle with shoulders wider than the pool table and eyes blacker than the eight ball. Rudy shared tips on hot-wiring cars and "finding" used hubcaps. His twin brother,

Ralph, was generous with dimes for the jukebox as long as no one cared if he sang along with Patsy Cline.

Jean and I harbored suspicions that some of the guys' seamier talents had occasionally landed them in hot water with the local sheriff, but we were also certain these skills would come in handy during later crucial moments in life. I could pick a lock with my eyes closed. Jean could start any vehicle with a battery and an engine in less than ten seconds flat.

The other regulars at *Wanda's* were men in their forties, fifties, and sixties who commandeered tables for pool and poker when the Home hunks got too busy listening to music and flirting with the older girls.

Claude, a gray-hair, sixty-five-year old giant who sported more wrinkles in his tanned face than a linen shirt in August, was the pool shark. He'd actually been Danny's mentor—a feat that, in our young eyes, made Claude undisputed King of the Cues. He told us he was originally from St. Paul and his college ring did have the University of Minnesota inscribed on it. Naturally, Jean and I put two and two together and came up with five.

"Wow! Come on, Claude. You can tell us. You're Minnesota Fats, right? What's Paul Newman really like?"

This always produced a large belly laugh from Claude's large belly. He'd smile, shake his head and leave us filled with awe over his prowess at the table and wonder about his true past.

One of our favorite regulars was "Jack" and that name is in quotes for a reason. "Jack" was a Willie Nelson lookalike and poker fanatic. His long gray hair was tamed into two braids, which rested well below his shoulder blades and were held back by a red bandana around his forehead. He had broad cheeks, a dark complexion and an accent straight out of a John Wayne-as-one-of-the-Texas-cavalry movie. He owned more turquoise and silver than a Santa Fe souvenir stand and told us to call him Jack because his Indian name was too long and unpronounceable. Jean once asked him what it meant in English.

His stoic response was, "He Who Walks by Moonlight in the Pond of the Great Spirit of the Joker."

Hamp happened to be serving a plate of fried chicken to Jack at the time. He leaned over the table, winked at Jean and me, and then snorted. "Horse Feathers."

I was never quite sure whether Hamp was telling us that Horse Feathers was Jack's real Indian name, promoting the Western wear store in town with the same name, or merely making a sarcastic comment.

Ronald Robert (Ronny Bob) was a local auto mechanic. One of the youngest of the regulars, he was good-looking even by the limited standards of teenagers believing anyone over age twenty-one is too old to be handsome. Except, of course, for Paul Newman. Medium height, wiry, with black curly hair and jade green eyes, Ronny Bob could have stepped right off the pages of any of our favorite movie magazines. He wore a ring on his left hand but I never heard anything about a Mrs. Ronny Bob, so there was always a question as to whether one existed, or he was a widower, or playing married to try to keep mobs of women away from him. Which didn't work. He was quiet, shy, and one whale of an amazing poker player. Watching him bluff out Jack or Claude in games of five-card stud or Texas Hold-em was an afternoon entertainment almost as fun as listening to the Beatles while stacking Paul McCartney trading cards—which somehow never got traded. Ronny Bob's technique in poker was akin to someone dancing a waltz in perfect rhythm, with grace and imperceptible but strong partnering.

Lamar was the ladies' man in that group. He sold door accessories, though how he ever made any money since it appeared he lived at *Wanda's* twelve hours or more a day was a mystery. Lamar had light brown hair that was gently graying at the temples, faded blue eyes, and tanned, crinkly skin from too much sun and cigarettes. He was equally adept at pool, poker, the Texas two-step and the Cotton-Eye Joe. The latter two he taught to Jean and me one afternoon before any players took their chairs for a marathon of cards. The five-and-dime counter girls always giggled when they talked to Lamar. So did the women encased in silk shirts and tight jeans who came from other parts of town to lunch at *Wanda's*. Jean and I assumed they weren't there to lap up the coconut cream pie and congratulated ourselves on our ability to see relationships through worldly eyes.

These older *Wanda's* habitués pretty much adopted Jean and me. They took great pains to entertain, and/or teach us, and we lapped up the attention and the knowledge.

Jean, especially, loved having five father figures (Hamp included) to fawn over her, tease her, and guide her into an attempt at becoming the best female poker player in Texas. She confided in me that since she wanted to be a foreign correspondent, and reporters in global locales were usually male, being an awesome poker player would be an asset in her future career. Unfortunately, she was wretched in the art of bluffing.

In the middle of a game, she'd direct a scowl my way. "Bonnie? Why are you folding so soon?"

"Because it's purty dadgummed obvious you've got a damned full house and I'd prefer to just hold on to my chips, thank you."

"But how can you know that? Hey! Are you cheating as well as swearing?"

"Jean, my brilliant, moronic friend. Your face is redder than the Queen of Hearts and you're giggling every time someone ups the bet. Hint, hint."

"Oh."

"Yeah. Oh."

Or: "How did y'all know I only had a pair of twos?" she'd inquire.

I'd calmly respond, "Maybe the fact that your eyes have gone around the table fifteen times in the last three seconds and you're sighing louder than a deflated balloon. I'm tellin' ya, if you want to hold your own with Dan Rather when you're reporting from the fields of Southeast Asia, you might consider drinking, burping or cigars as a male bonding activity. Not cards."

"Oh."

"Yeah. Oh."

Normally, a day at *Wanda's* was enough excitement for us, but one hot July afternoon that summer we grew bored with the routine.

"Bonnie, we're in a rut, " Jean stated. "We need to see what lies beyond *Wanda's*."

"I'm in. Do ya suppose Hamp has some nice bottles of soda he'd give us cheap?"

He did.

We left the pool game (I was losing anyway) and sauntered across the street to the five-and-dime. We spent about fifteen minutes trying out the latest in hair accessories, primping in front of the small mirror on the cosmetics counter. Jean's short curly brown hair looked ridiculous with a jeweled barrette. A black bandeau created too stark a contrast with my long blonde Patti Boyd 'do. We looked at each other, shuddered, and then put the clips and bands away. We tested the lipsticks, and decided that Jean's orange made her brown eyes yellow while red turned my fair skin corpse white. Cosmetics were out. We scanned the magazine rack for movie and teen idol news.

"Well, damn. These are the same magazines we saw last week," I complained.

"Yeah. I remember that story about the *Dave Clark Five's* wild party in Liverpool."

We sighed. Deep, world-weary sighs only sophisticated fourteen-year olds can sigh. Then, with a look of silent communication only best friends share, we knew.

The Great Fence beckoned.

I broke the silence. "Come on. Let's do it. Those wood are calling to us. *Jeeeeenie, Bonnnnieeeee*, come out and *plaaaaayyyy*."

"Will you quit? You're embarrassing me." She paused for approximately two seconds. "Okay. We're outta here."

We bought a few essentials, stuffed them into Jean's already bulging backpack, then left the security of the five-and-dime, *Wanda's*, and the strip mall parking lot to find adventure and with any luck—treasure.

Once we were at the Great Fence, we checked the area for possible authority figures who might put an end to our exploits before they began. Not a soul in sight. It was July in Texas. Only lunatics and teenagers even *considered* venturing outside. We scaled the fence with the ease of athletes, and then glanced down below.

The landing appeared to be a bit trickier than the going up process had been. Shrubs, prickly weeds, thorny vines awaited. We were undaunted. Our descent might not have exhibited grace but it was spirited and fast and we were over and on the ground standing in the small patch of what passed for a clearing.

"Ouch!" I removed a dry thorn from my arm. "Okay, Magellan. Where to?"

"Hmm." Jean pointed. "How 'bout going that way? It looks like there might have been a real path once."

"That way" was north. It quickly proved more challenging than we'd expected. Fallen branches blocked us, we tripped over roots. Vines grabbed, then clung, to our ankles. We persevered. Thirty minutes later, we were scratched, slightly bloody, hot, dirty, tired and very thirsty.

"Break!" I yelled.

"Shoot, Bonnie, you're a sissy."

"I am not! I have bloody badges of courage all over my knees and calves. But I can't be expected to find buried treasure in a weakened condition. I need rest. I need food. I need those sodas Hamp gave us no matter how hot they are now."

Jean stuck her tongue out at me, but dropped the backpack. "I'm only taking a break because if we don't eat the Snickers soon, they'll melt all over my bag."

"Yeah. Right. Hand 'em over."

We contentedly munched on chocolate (which had indeed melted) and drank warm sodas for the next ten minutes or so.

Then, with renewed strength and a major sugar high, we were ready to tackle the forest again. We started hiking through jungle-like territory. The growth of weeds now reached our knees. Dead tree limbs lay in every direction. My scratches were turning into bloody welts. Going back for a *Wanda's Special* was starting to have incredible appeal. I was about to suggest doing precisely that when suddenly we stumbled (literally) into a real clearing.

The dramatic change from the heat, the weeds, even dust, was immediate and slightly scary. Tall trees deflected searing rays of sunlight from entering, and there were no broken shrubs or patches of dried grass. Only one huge toppled tree barricaded the center. Finally, in this space, the earth itself felt cool— detached from the summer heat. The remains of long dead campfires lent stillness to the scene, as did empty tin cans and broken bottles.

The drop in temperature was welcome, and for some absurd reason filled us the hope that we were about to discover the find of the century.

Jean began hopping up and down. "What do you think? Diamonds? Pearls? Emeralds?"

"None of the above. Unfortunately, I don't see a nice case labeled 'priceless jewels' anywhere." I smiled.

"Well, poo, I'm disappointed. Not surprised, mind you, but disappointed."

Another good sit-down and relax session was clearly in order before we made the trek back to civilization. The fallen tree was tailor made for two semi-exhausted girls to plop in front of before devouring a picnic of chips and the remainder of soda that had gone from warm to nearly stove hot. We first scoured the area for any pesky rattlesnakes or sneaky copperheads who might have chosen this spot for their afternoon nap. No hissing or twitching could be heard or seen near the front of the tree but we were cautious. We tiptoed around the back to see if Mr. Rattles might be hiding in a hole.

We stopped.

The back side of the tree displayed a burnt portion, which had hollowed out a good chunk of the branch. I leaned down slowly in case that imagined snake lay in wait, and then popped my head back up.

"Hey. It's a trunk. A steamer trunk. It's dirty, it's chipped, and it's colorless. Looks *really* old. This is so cool!"

Jean leapt into the air, shrieking, "Yippee! Eureka! This is *it*. The moment we've been waiting for all our lives. Got to be a huge haul of treasure in there."

I joined her and we danced a little gig. "Rich! We're gonna be rich. We can go to England and meet the Beatles! Shit, we can go to England and *buy* the Beatles."

Our imaginations had reverted to the level of six-year olds. Not terribly smart six-year olds, at that.

Buried Treasure. Gold bullions left by Spanish pirates who doubtless had roasted marshmallows and hot dogs in this very spot three hundred years ago.

"Come on. Let's pull this sucker out."

I nodded. We squatted. We each grabbed a handle on the ends, and then carefully edged the trunk out of the hole in the tree. Simultaneously we sank to the ground. I made an attempt to wipe away the top layer of dust and dirt from the front of the trunk using the wad of sweaty tissues I'd cleverly concealed in my baseball cap.

"Hey, Jean. Check this out."

I pointed to the spot where I'd been diligently cleaning. Three letters stood out from beneath the grime. We both squinted and came up with the same conclusion. Initials. *M. D. H.*

"Far out! Let me think. M.D.H.," I mused. "Wait . . . Ha! I've got it. This is the chest of Morgan Death Heart, a fierce rapscallion from Madagascar. No. No. Better still. This belongs to one Mephistopheles Diablo Hernandez, ravisher of maidens and slayer of shipwrecked travelers from France. Ooh! Better! Manuel Diaz Harrigan from the Irish branch of Spain? Disowned by his Spanish cousins and sent to traverse the seas buckling swashes and also ravishing maidens."

Jean snickered, and then solemnly stated, "Your taste in fiction runs to pure trash. You do know this, I assume?"

"Who, me? Never. It's Mom's fault. She has a thing for Errol Flynn and Tyrone Power. Makes me sit up with her and watch their movies whenever Channel Eleven has them on. I know all the lines from *Captain Blood, The Sea Hawk and The Black Swan*. I'm extremely impressionable."

"You're extremely full of it. You're also wasting time. Let's crack this puppy and divvy up the spoils."

"Divvy up the spoils? And you call *me* full of it? What have you been watching? Early James Cagney and Edward G. Robinson?"

She ignored me. Wise move. She started tinkering with a heavy metal lock. The kind you use for your bike when you can't remember numbers for a combination padlock and have to use a key.

She pointed at the lock. "Dammit. This thing is not only locked up tight; it's rusted. We need your special skills. Bonnie the super picker."

I believe I've mentioned that, courtesy of some of my buddies at *Wanda's*, I'm a wiz at picking locks. Unfortunately, my organizational talents weren't as impressive, which is an embarrassed attempt to explain why I had no tools for the undertaking. But Jean had a mind like an accountant during tax season. With brilliant foresight, she'd included in her backpack items neither of us could be separated from for long—lipsticks, eye shadows, twenty-five Beatles trading cards (all of the fab four; not just Paul) rubber bands, Band-Aids, one nail file and a fist full of bobby pins. I grabbed one of the pins and, with intense concentration, began fiddling with the old padlock.

"Did you know that you sing *Mac the Knife* when you pick locks or break into things?" Jean stared at me with awe. "Where do you learn this stuff?"

"I come from a very musical family," I replied. "Everybody listens to something different. You should hear Pop when he's washing the car. Verdi to Van Morrison. Actually, he hoses to Verdi and waxes to Van. Pretty cool for an old guy. Now hush up and let me work."

I was just getting to the "Jenny Diver, Polly Peachum" verse when suddenly the lock gave way. I smiled up at Jean. "Ta, da! Gad, I'm good. They should bottle me and sell me."

"I have no nice response to that."

We each took a deep breath, grabbed an end of the lid, and slowly and carefully pried open the lid, then peered inside.

The trunk was filled with dozens of yellowed newspapers and clippings. They were stained, torn with edges frayed. Some appeared to have been chewed on by small rodents. Jean reached inside and gently picked up one of the lesser-destroyed papers. She lifted it out of the trunk, then immediately dropped it.

"It's cold," she gasped.

"That's loony! Newspapers don't hold heat or cold. Unless they're coming right off a press."

"Yeah, right, sure, fine. You touch it and tell me, Miss Know-It-All."

I did.

"It's cold." I shivered, dropped the paper and felt tiny rivers of sweat trickle down my neck. Jean and I stared at each other.

"I'm getting a bad case of the creeps," she whispered.

"Okay, look—we're being silly. Let's pull some of these out and see what's what. Probably advertisements for *Joe's Feed and Grain* or ladies lingerie or something, but we're still stuck on gold bullions and that's why we're imaging cold."

I delicately laid that paper on the ground. And read the headline.

Chicago Sun Times

Miss Mary Dale Howard Still Missing! Presumed Dead!

"Jean, take a look at this."

She peered over my shoulder. "Oh my God. This is weird. That date. July 20th, 1945. That's exactly twenty years ago yesterday. I mean the *very* day. Look at her name. Mary Dale Howard. *M.D. H.* Bet you anything this is her trunk."

Jean sank down and leaned against the tree.

I inhaled. "Jean, we're spooking ourselves. This is simply somebody's old trunk that was used for storage and . . . and . . . they filled it with whatever papers were lying around that week to protect, uh, like dishes and stuff. I bet we'll find broken cups and plates underneath."

"But why *that* particular newspaper with *that* story? What is a twenty-year old Chicago paper doing in Texas?"

"Because they moved down from Chicago, okay?"

"Bonnie, I'm really, really cold. I've got a bad feeling about this. Call it my future reporter's instincts but something is way wrong."

"All right, all right. Take a few breaths while I dig inside and find out what else is in here."

I began throwing decayed papers out and onto the ground, heedless of any destruction. I had to get them all out— fast. I was halfway through the pile when my hand touched something cold and sharp. I stopped, and then quickly stood up.

"What? Bonnie, talk to me. You look like you're going to either faint or throw up. There's no color in your face at all and that's going some with you."

"Let's leave. Go home and forget we ever found this here."

"What is it? Come on. Tell me!" Jean pushed me aside. "Oh."

We stared down at the ax nestled snugly between layers of newspapers. There appeared to be rust all over the blade. The wooden handle was chipped.

Jean began to shake. "I'm going to join you in being sick now."

"Damn. I see another headline." I carefully reached for a paper right under the ax, but was just as careful not to touch the tool. "Oh Jeez."

Chicago Sun Times

July 20th, 1945

AX MURDERER ON THE LOOSE!

Beneath the lurid headline was an even worse subheading.

Mary Dale Howard Believed Murdered in Chicago Hotel

"Looks like more papers under that—thing. That ax. We've got to somehow get it out and see what the others report."

Jean nodded. She scooped up her backpack; dumping what was left of our junk food. We used the dime store sack that had held the candy and chips to slowly lift the ax out of the trunk, and then set it on top of dead campfire ashes.

There were dozens more newspapers wadded up and jammed into every corner and crevice of the trunk. In a near frenzy, I began tossing them onto the ground. Most were torn and stained but all were clearly from Chicago and all were dated from July 20th through July 28th, 1945.

I glanced at Jean. "I need to know. I can't leave until I know."

"Yeah, me too. Let's do it. If I'm going to be the female Dan Rather, I need to learn to investigate without having to bring an airsick bag."

She began to smooth out a group of crumpled papers. I did the same. After perhaps five minutes of searching through now semi-flat pages, she poked my arm. "Bonnie. This one has quite a bit of information."

Her hands shook and her voice wasn't entirely steady as she read aloud.

CHICAGO SENTINEL   July 20th, 1945

"Chicago police are investigating what appears to be a homicide at the Allen Hotel. In response late last night to an anonymous tip, Officers John Riley and "Red" Mulligan broke into Room 453 of the downtown residence hotel where Mary Dale Howard had registered July 17th. They discovered what Officer Riley called 'a horrible, gruesome scene. One chair was broken, the wardrobe had been chopped into small pieces and there was blood everywhere.' The officers stated that articles of a personal nature had been strewn throughout the room. A handkerchief, stained with what appeared to be blood, embroidered with initials M.D.H. was discovered in a wastebasket. Police fear this could have been the spot where Mary Dale Howard, age nineteen and missing since July 19th, might have met with foul play. Jacob Howard, the young girl's uncle and guardian, identified the handkerchief as belonging to his niece. The officers told this reporter they are searching for the steamer trunk that held her belongings. A bellboy claims he remembers carrying such a trunk to Room 453 when Miss

Howard came to the Hotel on July 18th. Wanted for questioning by the police is Mr. Ezekiel Brown, age 31, a waiter at the Allen Hotel Diner, who has also not been seen since July 19th and who had been observed talking to Miss Howard on more than one occasion. This reporter learned that Mr. Brown is a suspect in the sla. . . ."

The rest of the sentence and paragraph had been torn.

The two of us sank down to the ground again.

"Jeez, Jean. He hacked her up. This Brown guy hacked her up and stuck her body in this trunk." I stared at my friend.

She stared back at me. "And exactly *how* did this trunk get here?"

"Are you serious? Easy. There were trains in Nineteen-forty-five. Lots of trains. That's how everybody traveled. Mom told me she rode on trains all through World War Two. Who would even notice one guy with a steamer trunk? He threw it on a train and came down here because no one would look for him in Texas."

"So are we being nuts here? I mean, you said it yourself, maybe this is only somebody's old trunk that they used for moving and it just happens to have this particular week's papers in it because they moved that week. Maybe they chopped wood and threw the ax inside."

I snorted. "Give me a break. For a future nosy newswoman, you sure are hiding from the truth. You saw it yourself. Look at the initials on this thing. Dammit, some maniac ax murderer from Chicago killed this Mary Howard, probably stuffed her body and the ax in the trunk, boarded a train to Texas, and kept the press clippings because he's a sicko." I paused. "I hate to bring this up, but what's really freaking me out is why the paper is so cold. Maybe I'm crazy to believe in stuff like this, but what if her spirit has stayed here all this time?"

Jean, wisely ignored the ghost reference. "Okay. Fine. Why was this girl at that hotel anyway?"

"Do I look like Miss Marple? Maybe she was running off to marry a soldier or maybe she wanted to be a chorus girl? What difference does it make? She got murdered!"

We both fell silent. A few moments passed. Finally, Jean grabbed my hand. "Do you think he buried her here? In these woods?"

"I've really been trying to avoid heading down that lane."

We continued to stare at the paper. The *Chicago Sentinel* edition had included a photo of Mary Dale Howard. The photo was terribly faded after twenty years but it appeared Mary had been quite pretty and looked so young she could have been in our class at school.

Suddenly, Jean snatched the paper off the ground. "Look at this. She was wearing a ring on her right hand. It kind of jumps right off the page. My God, it was really beautiful. Maybe a sapphire or garnet with diamonds in a circle?" She squinted. "How . . . odd. Bonnie, it reminds me . . ."

I barely heard her. I was busy listening to every motion made by every insect crawling by and becoming more and more nervous. "Jean, we need to go back now. I'll admit it. Big adventure girl is scared. What if Mr. Brown is lurking around waiting to hack us to bits?"

"Bonnie! Holy crap! Are you nuts? This Brown character is long gone. You're psyching yourself out over nothing."

The two of us got brave and cased the area for an elusive murderer. Silence.

I swallowed hard. "I still say let's go."

"Okay. Can we closed this stinkin' trunk first?" Jean asked.

"Definitely."

We slammed the lid down, and then hurriedly threw our belongings back into Jean's pack. We ran out of the clearing. We didn't notice or feel the cuts on our legs, the branches whipping across our faces. What had taken forty or more minutes to hike into took less than fifteen to exit. We didn't stop running 'til we reached the Great Fence. The specter of Ezekiel Brown and his ax followed us the entire trip back. We didn't even begin to breathe normally until we'd actually climbed over the fence and plopped down on a bench outside Jean's dormitory.

We sat there for about twenty minutes without speaking. Despite the heat of the July afternoon, I shivered with cold. Jean turned to me, then spoke quietly. "I keep seeing that ring. I can't stop thinking about it."

"Yeah. It's weird—I mean, how clearly it showed up in the newspaper picture."

She shook her head. "It's not that. It's . . ..

I interrupted her. "I know. Shoot, Jean, it makes her *real.* She wore that ring with pretty dresses to match the color. She flirted with guys. She went to movies and drank sodas at five-and-dime counters and . . . then. . . she met Ezekiel Brown. I wonder how he tricked her into going with him to—wherever."

Jean brightened. "Maybe that's what happened."

"What?"

"Maybe she never was killed. Maybe it's all a romance and we're reading nasty things into an old trunk because the newspapers at that time thought this was a murder. But maybe she and Ezekiel fell in love and just took off together? Packed her trunk with her belongings, came to Texas. Didn't need the trunk after they moved and he just threw an ax in there because it was rusty?"

"Good grief. I'm glad you're planning on being a reporter because as a fiction writer, you stink."

She glared at me. "What's the matter with my story?"

"Oh, how about the fact that the papers said this Brown was a suspect in something else? How about the way the room was messed up and the wardrobe chopped up and her bloody handkerchief in the trash, and she didn't tell her uncle she was going anywhere?"

"Oh. Yeah. Didn't think about that."

I shuddered. "Plus there's also the cold we felt. I mean, I'm not sure I even believe in ghosts, but if anyone has reason to haunt that trunk, it's Mary Dale Howard."

We sat in silence a few more minutes. Then I stood. "I hate to do this, but I've got to get home. Pop's giving Brian a driving lesson tonight and I promised to go along with them."

"Why? Didn't you say Brian was a lousy driver?"

"Yep. He is. But Brian says when I go with them Pop doesn't yell at him as much. He's very sensitive."

Jean smiled. "Yeah. Real sensitive. All six-five, All-Star offensive tackle of brother Brian. Not buying it, Bonnie."

I grinned at her. "Well, there *is* the added perk that Pop lets *me* drive a little when he can't stand Brian's speedway mentality. Listen, try not to think about what we found. After all, it's twenty years ago and what can we do anyway? Call the cops and say, 'there's an old trunk in the woods filled with papers and an ax and we think a murderer left it there in Nineteen-forty-five? I'm sure that'd go over really well." I paused before adding, "You want me to walk you back to your dorm?"

"Nah. I'm going to sit here a bit longer." She took a deep breath. "That ring."

"What about it?'

"Didn't it remind you a little of the bracelet my mom left me?"

"Oh. Jeez. I don't know. You never wear any jewelry, so I don't really remember." I glanced at my watch again. "Want to go in and check? We could hurry."

"Nah, it's okay. It would be a really bizarre coincidence if they came from the same jeweler or something since as far as I know my parents were never in Chicago. But they might have been. I'm probably imagining things. The paper didn't exactly have the best photo and we were getting so spooked I'm seeing shadows where there aren't any."

I hesitated. "I can stay for awhile. Really. I just need to call my folks and tell them I'm not going to be Brian's buffer for the lesson tonight."

Jean shook her head. "No. It's fine. See ya tomorrow?"

"Sure. I didn't get my slice of *Wanda's* pie today, and I'm not sure I can get through the rest of the week without it."

We hugged each other. I unlocked my bike from the rack near the front entrance of the Home, and then pedaled off. Brian and my dad were waiting for me, so I dumped the bike in our garage, and then hopped into the car. Pop and I suffered through Brian's horrible driving for awhile, then decided to call it quits and get some ice cream. We made it back home around nine p.m.

I kicked off my sneakers, and trotted into the family room to call Jean. Mom stopped me.

"Jean phoned and left a message for you. She said to call her at *Wanda's*."

"That's it?" I asked.

"Hang on, sweetie. Let me decipher my handwriting. Okay. Here's the full message. She said something about being sure about a ring and that she was going to put on her reporter's cap and ask a few subtle questions."

My entire body went still except for the blood pulsing up to my brain. "Wait. She said she's going to go ask questions at *Wanda's* about that ring?"

Mom squinted again at her scribbled notes. "Yep. Let me see. Something about catching a bus? No, that's not right. The word is 'bluff.' She's planning to catch someone by a bluff? That makes no sense either."

"It does to me." I began to babble. "Jean can't bluff. She's terrible. She's going to end up in trouble. We've got to get over there. To *Wanda's*. Now!"

My parents have always joked about the big dramatic streak coursing through my veins, but they also know me well enough to tell when I'm terrified of something real. *This* was real. We raced to *Wanda's* faster than Brian ever imagined driving. I gave the short story version of the afternoon's events and Jean's preoccupation with the picture of Mary Dale Howard and the ring and how she thought the ring looked like some jewelry her mom had left her, but we couldn't figure out the how or why of the similarities.

All seemed normal at *Wanda's*. Except, there was no Jean. All the older regulars were there. Well, everyone but Lamar. I tried to stay calm.

"Hey, hi, Jack, everybody. Uh. Have you guys seen Jean? Or Lamar?"

Jack glanced up from his cards. "They were both here coupla hours ago. We was playin' a few hands."

Hamp slid out from behind the bar and walked over to join us at the poker table. "What's the matter?"

I inhaled. "Did Jean happen to ask Lamar anything about a ring?"

Claude gave me a sharp look. "Jean did mention somethin' bout a ring, but not just to Lamar. She was playing five-card stud with us and kinda teasin' bout Jack's turquoise and my old school ring. I seem to recall she said to Lamar how she'd like to see his pinkie ring right side up. You know, he doesn't always wear it, but when he does have it on, he keeps the stone turned down, ever since Hamp was buggin' him one time about a pinkie ring with a sapphire lookin' funny on anyone who wasn't a gangster. Anyway, I wouldn't't've thought much bout it but she kept heavin' that sigh she does when she's tryin' to bluff so I did wonder why she was interested."

"Claude, what happened after she asked about his ring?" I asked.

Claude paused. He laid his cards down on the table. He looked at me, at my mom and dad, and then stood. I'd forgotten how really huge he was. Six-six. Even bigger than my brother.

"Well, seems as if Lamar said he'd be glad to show it to her tomorrow, but he didn't have it with him tonight. And we all played a couple of hands of five-card stud. Then Jean said it was late and she figured she needed to be gettin' on home. We waved goodbye. I didn't think about it at the time, but Lamar got up not long after she left. He never came back to start a new game."

"Oh, dear God."

Everyone stared at me. Time to go into explanation number two about the afternoon's events and Jean's questions about the ring and a possible relation to her mom's bracelet. I told the men what Jean and I had discovered in the woods behind the State Home and my growing gut feeling that she thought Ezekiel Brown might have morphed into Lamar because his pinkie ring looked a lot like the ring in the picture in the paper. The ring that had belonged to Mary Dale Howard. My dad asked to use Hamp's phone as soon as I began my tale this time, and called the dorm to ask if Jean was safely ensconced in her room. "No" was the answer from her suitemates. No one had seen her since she and I left the Home this afternoon.

The next few hours were like being smothered in nitrous oxide before a tooth extraction. That horrible sense of loss of control and floating above the ground.

Police came. Police questioned. I told my story for the third time, feeling pain even through the numbness.

I escorted the police to the clearing behind the Home.

The trunk was gone. The newspapers and the ax were gone. Remnants of a backpack were stuck to the branches.

And my best friend was gone.

I never went back to *Wanda's*. I endured a few more interrogations by the police, but there was nothing to add to what they already knew. Although, in August, one of the officers who'd first arrived at *Wanda's* the night Jean disappeared did tell me he'd done some searching into Mary Dale Howard's disappearance and her family background, and made a startling discovery pertaining to Jean. He'd learned that Jean's mom's maiden name was Howard. Mary Dale Howard had been Jean Rose Callahan's aunt. The same cold that had enveloped me when we opened that damned, doomed trunk overtook me the instant he relayed the information. I had to believe Mary Dale's spirit had somehow been . . . released that day, although the justice denied her in life remained unresolved in death.

When school started in September I kept pretty much to myself. My classmates nibbled at me for a month wanting to know all the details about the fence, and the trunk and Jean, but when a twister hit the city in October and took out a section of downtown, the events of the summer were forgotten, and I was left in peace.

Three years later, I graduated from high school. Went to college in Austin. I took a double major in drama and journalism.

I never married Paul McCartney. Never went to England. Senior year of college I ran into my old crush from *Wanda's*—Mike, the good-looking Ping Pong champ. He was in Austin attending law school. We got married right after we both graduated and we moved to El Paso. He's with the district attorney's office there. I'm entertainment critic for the newspaper. I review movies and plays and concerts and television. We have three kids. A boy named Rudy, and twin girls named Jean Rose and Mary Dale.

Mike, the kids and I drove to town last week to visit my folks. Today the whole tribe went to the zoo. I pleaded a headache and drove out to the State Home.

An iron fence still surrounds the Home on three sides. To the east, once elegant 19th Century homes that were shells of poverty in the Sixties have been destroyed. Storage facilities dot entire blocks. The west side still borders 18th Street, but *Wanda's* has been replaced by a fast food taco joint and the Shopping Center now bears the name of one of America's largest discount department stores. A small opening to the south of the fence leads visitors past neat grounds to the dormitories. The bench under the light post still looks the same as it did when Jean and I sat and discussed our findings in the woods while she pondered whether or not she'd seen a ring on the finger of a man we'd once thought of as a friend. Behind the Home to the north where once overgrown shrubs, weeds and dead trees made up the landscape, tract houses now stand. The Great Fence still has a *No Trespassing* sign on it and there's a dirt road separating the Home from the new houses beyond.

I stood by the sign for a long time before pulling out the newspaper I'd stuffed into my large carryall bag and re-reading the small article no once else had seemed to notice this morning, regarding a missing teenager from a small town in Montana. Sadly, girls *do* go missing, but most of the time their disappearances aren't given space in newspapers more than a thousand miles away. Yet a Montana reporter had found certain aspects of the case intriguing, and consequently, so had the owners of the local paper here in Texas.

The Montana reporter, Jason Nesbitt, noted that the missing girl, fourteen-year-old Tracey Charlene Simmons, and her friend, Sharon Pressler, had spent much of July 19th exploring an area in the thick woods not far from town. According to Nesbitt, Shannon Pressler explained when questioned by police, that she and Tracey were simply being silly, looking for buried treasure, eating junk food, and avoiding possible encounters with copperheads, when they literally stumbled across a very old steamer trunk.

They managed to pry the lid open. They found a very rusted ax lying among a large, but faded assortment of Texas newspapers dated July 20th, 1965.

All the headlines provided the same basic story: *"Search Continues for Missing State Home Girl!"*

Shannon had additionally told police Tracey had wildly claimed the newspapers were cold, even though the July afternoon temperatures were in the mid-90s. She'd become oddly obsessed with the photo displayed in each of the old Texas papers, featuring the girl who'd gone missing twenty years earlier, a fourteen-year-old named Jean Rose Callahan.

I knew that photo. I'd given it to the police. It's the one where Jean is holding a dog named Lugnut, who belonged to her best friend. Her wrist clearly displays a bracelet she inherited from a mother she never knew. The bracelet once matched a ring belonging to Mary Dale Howard. A ring that had briefly flashed across five cards one night when Ezekiel Brown sweetened the pot during a poker game in a diner called *Wanda's* barely three months before two girls went exploring.

Today is July 20th, 1985.

Twenty years gone.

And Tracey Charlene Simmons, feeling cold where cold should have been impossible to feel, had vanished.

END

Labor Day / Ladies Night

"Is that a parking space over there?"

"Where?"

"There! Next to the Lexus."

"What? Ginny, are you blind? That's not a Lexus. That, my dear, is a classic, 1966 Corvette. Cherry red. Sexy."

"Hey!" I yelled. "Lemme see. I've always wanted a 'Vette."

Two voices chorused as one, "*No.*"

Nuts. The blindfold stayed firmly in place over my eyes. Ginny and Sandra seemed determined it would remain there. They'd even tied my hands behind my back with a scarf so I couldn't remove it.

Kidnapped by my best friends. Hog-tied and veiled. The felonious deeds had begun around three this afternoon when the pair arrived at my apartment and asked me to close my eyes for a "surprise." Suddenly, I was being stuffed into the back seat of Ginny's car for Stage One of the crime.

We'd driven to a day spa where I'd been treated to what my friends referred to as "the Full Monty" at special Labor Day prices. My bob was cut into a shag and auburn highlights woven into my hair. I sipped on herbal tea and devoured almond cookies for three minutes, and then it was on to the steam and

moisturizing facial. Next, a large, Viking-accented blonde

plopped me into a chair and redid my face. Wine-colored eye shadow, wine-colored blush, wine-colored lipstick, and a ton of rich black mascara. For the two seconds I was allowed to glimpse the finished product in the mirror, I was pleased and even ready to cough up some money for product. Ginny and Sandra firmly said, "No" and slapped down the plastic for all the wine-colors and mascara.

Ginny and Sandra then let me retie the blindfold myself lest they inadvertently mess up the cosmetics, but made me promise I wouldn't pull it off.

We drove to an Italian restaurant in downtown Dallas, and spent several hours spent digging into salad, garlic bread, lasagna, fettuccini and cannolis. We left, groaning but blissful. Again, I was guided into the car and we headed south.

When the *News at Ten* blasted over the radio, I started getting nervous. Ginny and Sandra kept giggling. That made me more nervous. Ginny eased the car to a crawl when she spotted the Corvette.

"Hey, guys. May I please take this thing off? Pretty please?"

"Nope."

I sighed. Nervous and clueless about my present location. All I knew is that we were somewhere near interesting vehicles. The criminals gently eased me out of the car and kept me from toppling to the ground. Suddenly I could hear the voices of women. Tons of women. Chattering, chirping, giggling women.

"Ooh. I think I've got it," I chortled. "The Highland Park late night fashion show. Labor Day thing, right? I remember reading that they'd have all the latest from *Neiman's* and *Lillie Rubin* and *Lord & Taylor* and *Cachet.* This is cruel, ladies. Gorgeous clothes do me no good now."

Sandra snorted. "*Cold.* Cold, cold and skating into freezing. Give up, Mimi. Just hang on to us and all will be revealed."

My captors led me inside a building filled with the odor of perfume and menthol cigarettes. They grabbed me before I could stumble over a chair. Not until I was safely ensconced in my seat did Ginny rip off the blindfold.

I was in a bar. A bar reminiscent of sets for bad Seventies disco movies. Tiny tables had been set up on both levels of the bar. A runway filled center space.

Each tiny table was encircled with chairs filled with women. Women drinking out of foo-foo glasses decorated with pink umbrellas. Women drinking out of shot glasses. Women drinking out of beer bottles. If this was a fashion show, it clearly did not involve *Neimans*, or *Lord & Taylor* or even *Cachet.* Definitely not *Lillie Rubin.*

Ginny grinned at me. "Any guesses?"

"A lesbian disco?"

"Mimi, you're *such* a hoot. Nope. You're in *Big Bertha's.*"

I stared at Ginny. Clearly she had just lost her mind. Big Bertha's is short for *Big Bertha's Bare Babes Bar*. Located between Dallas and Red Oak, it's a notorious strip club. For men.

"I am *so* confused."

Ginny grabbed a passing waiter by the back of his shirt. "Gin and tonic, light beer for the lady in blue and . . . " She pointed toward me. "Perrier with lime for this one. Just keep 'em coming."

Sandra gestured around our surroundings. "Tonight is *Big Bertha's* Labor Day Charity bash amateur strip show. For ladies only. We are about to be entertained by hunky men who *do* have real jobs but tonight are flashing their buff bods in front of the rabid women you see everywhere."

My eyes opened wide. "You're kidding. And you dragged me here—why?"

The efficient waiter set our drinks in front of us before she could respond. I opened my Perrier, poured it into a frosted glass, squeezed the entire lime inside, and began to drink with ladylike sips.

Sandra took a large swig from her bottled beer. "Mimi, my buddy. Have you not been complaining that your hormones are raging? Did you not tell me you were watching some old Australian movie to see Hugh Jackman's butt? Did you not tell me you were watching the DVD of the movie version of *A-Team* to see Bradley Cooper's chest? Did you not tell me . . .?"

I interrupted before any more private fantasies were broadcast all over *Big Bertha's*. "But . . . a strip club catering to men?"

Ginny answered. "It's not a strip club catering to men. It's a strip club *normally* used by men that is now being catered by women watching men strip."

Sandra and I stared at her. I nodded. "Thank you, Ginny, for that semi-clarified elucidation."

"Huh?"

"I forgot. No words with more than one syllable."

She threw her tiny pink umbrella at me. It had been floating in a gin and tonic, not a Mai Tai, which seemed to me an obvious breach of good taste, but I declined to point this out. I had a suspicion *Big Bertha's* wasn't known for cultural amenities.

I looked around the club again, and then back at my friends. Good friends. While tying the blindfold over my eyes earlier this afternoon, they'd stated that all they wanted in return for their "surprise" was my heart's undying gratitude for enjoying what they clearly believed would be a memorable experience.

Ginny had added, "I want to see that same look you had when you won those tickets to France three years ago. That expression of pure joy."

Pure joy was the furthest thing from my mind right now. A twinge of pain sliced through me. "Ouch."

Sandra looked concerned. "Mini-Mimi?"

"Yeah. For about the ninetieth time this week. The doc calls it Braxton Hicks contractions. I call it bloody damned painful. At any rate, baby girl is either telling me she's bored and ready to pop out, or the cannolis were good and she wants more, or simply cheering *'Bring on the hunks!'*"

A male voice suddenly blasted across the club through huge speakers attached to a catwalk above. "Ladies! Welcome to *Big Bertha's* Labor Day Charity Event *'Bucks for Bucks.'* Remember, all tips the dancers make go directly to the Dallas ASPCA. Bertha is also matching your cover. Relax, enjoy yourselves and checkout the sexiest men this side of the Trinity River. Now, give it up for—*El Zorro.*"

Hoots and hollers greeted him. The sound of salsa music bellowed forth as Ricky Martin's *"Livin' La Vida Loca"* heralded the entrance of a masked man who popped out from behind a curtain and proceeded to strut down the center aisle, shedding hat, cap and shirt. A brown torso shimmied as Ricky led him "upside, inside, and out." A sword flashed under the lights and six women rushed the stage, eager to impale themselves.

This was great. For the first time in almost a year, I was having fun.

"Mini-Mimi," as Ginny and Sandra referred to the eight-and-a-half-month old fetus inside me, had been a source of joy mixed with pain since her conception. Barely a week after I'd discovered I was pregnant, I'd gotten word that my husband, Darren, had died while conducting a research project in Brazil for the University of Dallas. I'd dealt with funeral directors, life insurance agents, and distraught family members in between check-ups with my obstetrician and crying jags over the loss of a man twenty-five years my senior, who, while not the steamy passion of my life, had been a very kind and very good friend to me. I was thrilled, but terrified, to be carrying the baby.

A guy in a camel blazer, tan slacks, with black horn-rimmed glasses perched on his nose, came strutting out onto the stage, interrupting my short reverie.

Ginny screeched in horror. "Oh my God!"

"What? He's kinda cute."

"He's *also* Ted Dreenen. He teaches science at my school. Right down the hall from me. I can't believe this."

The announcer was announcing. "Here's—*The Chessman.*"

I had to admire Ted's taste in music. The song he'd chosen was *One Night in Bangkok* from the musical *Chess*. Ted used the slow intro to arrange a chessboard smack in the center of the stage.

The music kicked up. Ted whipped off the glasses and the blazer. A wiry body was visible under the white shirt. He twirled the chessboard over his head, then hurled it offstage—thankfully away from the audience. Squeals. The shirt came off. The pants came off. Brown spandex trunks kept him beach decent, but didn't hide much. The man was gorgeous. He also moved like a professional. I teach dance at my own studio in East Dallas and I'd been a member of the Dallas Ballet. This guy had leaps, turns and footwork that rivaled anything I'd seen in the six years I'd spent in the company. I considered tossing my business card onstage to ask him to call if he was interested in having me arrange an audition.

Ginny kept moaning. "I'm never going to be able to face him in the hall again. And I have to work with him on the school art and science fair this week." She gasped. "Wow! Did you see that?"

"That" was a hip thrust eliciting a shower of bills from the audience.

Ginny's mouth dropped to her chest. I leaned over and shut her jaw, then snapped my fingers in front of her face. "Well, gee, Gin, looks like he's checking you out. Check and 'mate'?"

He was indeed smiling at her. Ginny blushed like a twelve-year old caught in the choir loft with an erotic novel. Ginny would go broke if she continued throwing twenty-dollar bills at the science teacher with the biologically gifted body as though they were quarters. I grabbed her hand. "Ginny! You've just tossed about two-hundred bucks up there."

"I have?" She looked astonished.

"You have."

"Oh well. It's for a good cause. Uh. I love animals."

Sandra tried unsuccessfully to smother a fit of laughter. She pointed an accusatory finger at Ginny. "You've never even owned a goldfish. What are you talking about? Animals? Can we say liar, here? Sheesh."

I threw a slightly damp napkin at Sandra. "Leave her alone. The girl's in love. *L. U. V.* Big time."

The next act up featured a man mimicking the old heavy metal rocker Marilyn Manson. Black and white make-up obscured his features, but his face wasn't the focal point anyway. He'd poured a deliciously sculpted body into a black and white cat suit tighter than pantyhose. The body parts revealed under the spandex were—well—splendidly exhibited. I waited to see what music "Marilyn" would use.

An unmistakable bass riff sounded throughout the club. The *"Bertha Butt Boogie."*

Sandra howled and hiccupped simultaneously. Ginny choked on her drink. My ribs ached from laughing.

We watched, wide eyed, as "Marilyn" hopped around the stage demonstrating pelvic thrusts with each thump of that bass guitar. His rhythm wasn't the best I'd ever seen (actually he was barely matching the beats) but he was definitely enthusiastic. He added pyrotechnics to the routine, finishing with a huge flash lighting up the edge of the stage.

I was petrified the entire bar would ignite. I could only imagine the special bulletin on Channel Five. *Hysterical Pregnant Ballerina Carried Out of Burning Bar by Naked Men! More News at Eleven!*

My eyes were tearing from Marilyn's last smoke-filled combustion, and I nearly missed the lithe, dark-haired gentleman dressed in firefighter regalia who rushed out and doused the flame with a fire extinguisher. A cheer rang out, followed by wolf-whistles from at least three middle-aged ladies seated four tables away from us.

The announcer stated," Now, for anyone still feeling only mildly warm, here's *Mr. Blaze* to get you flaming!"

The music changed to Donna Summer's *"Hot Stuff."*

"Hoppin' Hot Tamale!" I exhaled.

"Mimi? Did you just say what I think you said?"

"I did. And I'll say it again. Hoppin' Hot Tamale! That man alone is worth the admission price. He can light my pilot any day of the week."

For a moment, I thought he'd heard me. His neck whipped around toward our table and chocolate brown eyes gazed directly into mine. I gulped. Beads of sweat trickled down my back. Forget trickle. Go with gushed. The tablecloth I was clutching with increasingly damp hands would be soaked within seconds if this didn't stop.

Ginny tapped me. "Look. He's staring at you and he hasn't missed a step."

I grinned. "He may not be missing steps, but he's fast missing that outfit."

He unlooped his suspenders, and ripped off a dark-colored shirt to reveal a tanned, nicely muscled chest. His belt dropped.

I grabbed my water and drank the entire bottle. When I glanced up again, he was still looking my direction, the belt was resting on the floor and the trousers were easing down.

"Mimi, he just winked at you."

"He did not. He winked at everyone. Sandra? He's awfully near our table, isn't he?"

Sandra roared. "Honey, any closer and he'd be *on* the table. Mimi, you've definitely made a conquest."

I grimaced. "Yeah, right. Some conquest. I can't even stand up to put money in his briefs. I'd tip over from Mini-Mimi. Which would doubtless extinguish *his* fire." I paused. "Oh my Great-Aunt Agnes."

Hot Tamale's pants were off. Red, spandex briefs covered the essentials. Barely.

I threw another wadded up napkin at Sandra. This one was ringing wet from the Perrier I'd spilled seconds before while trying to adjust my position and not let Hot Tamale *Mr. Blaze* see how much I was affected by his performance. "You're drooling, Sandy-girl. Right down your chinny-chin-chin."

She absently wiped away the drool. "Sue me. He's a fox."

I felt absurdly jealous. I was sitting in a bar with at least a hundred other women looking at a man as near naked as one could get before removing that last, vital strip of cloth. And I didn't want anyone else seeing him. Crazy. I'd never met him but felt territorial. I wondered if pregnancy hormones causing the heat flowing in my body were responsible for love at first sight.

I grabbed another bottle of water and polished it off as I watched Mr. Blaze strut, bump and grind. Every movement seemed aimed at me. I turned as red as his briefs.

Then he was gone. I began to daydream about being rescued from a tree by the fireman, rather like a cat. I started to purr. Sandra nudged me— hard.

"Mimi. Look up there quick and tell me I'm hallucinating. Crap. I'm not. I cannot believe this. I'm going to kill him. Where's my gun?"

A tom-tom rhythm vibrated throughout the bar. I recognized *"Indian Reservation,"* the old Sixties hit by Paul Revere and the Raiders. I first thought that Sandra, being part Cherokee, might be annoyed they were using the song to strip. Then I realized one of the two guys dancing in war paint and leather chaps with ankle bracelets and headbands looked very familiar.

Sandra's husband of nine years was shaking everything he had in front of his astonished wife.

"That's Scott!" I yelled.

"I *know*. You think I don't recognize those legs and chest? Plus, he's the only lawyer in Dallas who wears his hair in a long braid."

"What the hell is Scott doing up there? And who's with him?"

"Vernon. His brother. He doesn't even *live* in Dallas."

"Whoa. Very interesting."

Sandra kept muttering. "I'm going to kill him. Drag his naked butt home, tie his braid to the bed, and scalp him."

I laughed. "Watch out, girl. There's lots of ladies here who look more than willing to tie that braid themselves. Probably to their little fingers. I can feel the lust from here."

Sandra snorted. "I should tell them at home the only briefs *I* see are those from the law firm. Some sexy Cherokee."

She was smiling. I had a feeling there'd be a good time on the reservation tonight.

The tribesmen finished with a flurry of ripped loincloths replaced by giant feather headdresses. Big Bertha, or whoever'd programmed the order of dances for the evening, possessed a sense of humor. The "Indians" were followed by a black-leather clad cowboy with black belt, hat and bandana. Theme music from the movie version of *Wild, Wild West* filled the bar. The cowboy looked somewhat like Will Smith, who'd played Jim West in the film. He tossed his gun holster to a table of middle-aged fans, and began executing some terrific karate kicks in skimpy black leather booty shorts, causing a near heart attack from a red-faced woman opposite us.

With Ginny mooning about her science teacher, me mooning about an anonymous firefighter, and Sandra trying to get over watching her spouse and brother-in-law mooning the audience, our trio stayed relatively quiet.

I hardly noticed the last few acts, although I enjoyed the music, especially when a hip-hopping stripper gyrated to the M.C. Hammer tune, *"Can't Touch This."* The audience was inclined to do the opposite. Women were jumping out of their seats and storming the stage, only being held back by two ridiculously large bouncers who looked like they'd taken the day off from their normal jobs as wrestling champions. I didn't care. I was too busy trying not to wince from the pain my little darling was inflicting on me. She appeared to be choreographing a routine in my abdomen, complete with high kicks and boxing jabs, while executing a break-dance spin on her tiny head.

The club closed at two a.m. We all decided to wait 'til the crowd thinned before trying to push me and my stomach through. I had no desire to battle a mob. So, Sandra, Ginny and I simply sat back and ordered another drink, enjoying each other's company.

After about twenty minutes of waiting, Scott and Vernon strolled over to our table to proudly display their tips of over seven hundred dollars—all for charity.

I looked for my hot tamale fireman. Not around. I figured he'd settled up with Bertha, and then gone home. I almost started sobbing. Amazing how attracted I was to him. Stupid, but I swore it was real nonetheless. Not out-of-control pregnancy hormones but a strange yet honest pull to the man. I'd never felt that way in my life. How can one fall in love at first sight with a man who's shaking his all for a group of screaming females in a dark club? Answer? Damned easily.

I could feel my stomach distending with the water I'd drunk. "Y'all excuse me? I'd better use the little dancer's room before we leave."

Sandra gave me a quick hug. "Ginny will take you home. I'm leaving with Mr. Tribal Heat here. After all, the criminal portion of the night is over."

"Criminal? We're of age, ya know. We have every right to be in a bar watching semi-naked men. Oh, wait. You're talking about the mommy napping of little me. Definitely criminal and I *will* get you back for this."

She grinned. She knew I'd had a terrific time.

I staggered toward the ladies room near the rear exit, did my business, and had started smearing soap on my hands when my spine suddenly felt as though one of Scott's tomahawks had sliced it. The pain was intense and debilitating. I hung onto the sink for support. Water rushed out of me and cascaded across the floor.

I stayed rooted in that position for at least five minutes. Hopefully, Ginny would come for me. If not, I might be giving birth on the tile floor of the restroom of a topless bar. Not good.

The door opened. Ginny.

"Hey, Gin. Uh. I have a problem."

"I'll say you do. Did your water break?" she asked brightly.

I growled. "No, Ginny, I'm hanging out in here rehearsing a pole dance routine using the sink for leverage. Of course, my friggin' water broke! *Ouch! Oh, Holy Mama!*"

"What?"

"I think I'm having major contractions. As in 'coming soon, Mama'. Either that or Mini-Mimi is auditioning for the *Rockettes*. In spiked tap shoes."

I groaned. I cursed. I groaned again. I cursed louder. "Ginny! Help!"

"Oh, Lordy. Are you really in labor? What can I do? Wait. Let's get you out of here. This is no place for a baby."

"You got that right."

Ginny eased my hands off the sink and helped me out of the restroom.

The club had emptied. It appeared only Ginny and I were left. She gently lowered me to my chair. I gripped the sides hard, then screamed.

Ginny turned white. "I hate to sound like Miss Prissy, but I truly know 'nothin' 'bout birthin' babies.'"

A rich baritone spoke behind my left ear. "I do. Part of emergency training. I don't just dance as a firefighter—it's my day job. I need a cell phone. Mine's in my car."

Ginny jumped up. "I left mine in the car, too. I'll run get it."

"Ma'am, why don't you check the front office first and tell Bertha it's an emergency and you need the landline? I'll stay with the young lady here. Should be faster."

I looked up through my wall of pain and saw *Mr. Blaze,* now clothed in jeans, boots and an olive-colored shirt. The incongruous thought hit me that this particular shade of green brought out the rich brown of his eyes and made his hair even darker. Incongruous, because I was simultaneously biting off a howl.

He took my hands in his. "It's okay. Yell all you want. Considering how loud the music was tonight, who can hear anyway?" He smiled reassuringly at Ginny and me. "Bertha's still in the office, counting loot. Call 9-1-1 and all will be well."

Ginny nodded. "Thanks. I'll be right back."

She ran. *Mr. Blaze* leaned in. "Breathe. Now. Okay. Want to try another?"

I woofed. "I'm stable. For now. Nothing major kicking in. Maybe it's a false alarm?"

"Water break yet?"

"Yep."

"Probably the real thing, then. But there's a hospital not too far away. Most of the time labor takes hours and hours. You'll be fine."

"Thanks."

We stared at each other. I let out another breath. "So - what's your name? Other than *Mr. Blaze* or Hoppin' Hot Tamale?" I bit my lip, this time out of humiliation. "I am *so* sorry. I can't believe I said that. The tamale thing. And I'm absolutely sober thanks to the kid here."

He laughed, showing nice teeth. "Hot Tamale, huh? Actually, I like it. So," he teased, "Exactly how much did my routine rake in from you and your two buddies?"

He *had* noticed. Otherwise why mention our trio?

"Oh, you did all right. Only because we *love* animals."

He grinned, then said, with an exaggerated Texas drawl, "Wa'll, thank ya, ma'am. Ah appreciate ever l'il cent." He dropped the accent. "I truly won't see a penny. When Bertha says charity, she means it. But this is a great cause. I got my collie through a rescue effort by ASPCA. I didn't mind flashing some skin for puppies."

"You flashed quite nicely, I must say." I paused, "So, what's your real name? If you don't mind my asking?"

"Mark. Mark Winter. You?"

"Me what?"

"Name? I'd like to know who's breaking the bones in my hand." He winked at me.

"Oh *damn!* I'm *so* sorry. Another minor wave just hit and I went under. Your hand was all that was keeping me afloat. And I'm Mimi Mihalik."

"Pretty."

"Thanks." I gasped as another wave threatened to drown me. Major. I panted as Mark calmly urged me to breathe. "Trying! Really. But I think I'd rather wail right now."

I did. He didn't even flinch. Heck, the man went into burning buildings every other day or so. The screams of a woman barely one hundred pounds pre-baby was no big deal. He stroked my sweating forehead. The wave subsided.

"Uh, Mimi, I forgot to ask your friend to call your husband."

I sighed. "My husband died eight months ago. Didn't even know I was pregnant." Tears welled up in my eyes.

"My God! You have my sympathy. Um, what happened? Do you mind talking about it? Might keep your focus away from the pain."

"Sure. Anything to avoid pain. And it's an interesting tale. Really. Darren was an ornithologist. Studied birds, you know? Anyway, he got this great grant to go off and observe the nesting habits of the great white peacock or something down in South America. All was going well until . . . one morning he was jotting down all his notes from the day before and he was eating a trail mix with cranberries and nuts and seeds. Right next to his snack, he'd also prepared a treat for the birdies with *china*berries and nuts and seeds. Got a handful of the wrong stuff. Poisonous to humans. Knocked him right off his perch. So to speak."

Mark struggled to suppress a grin, but failed. "I'm *truly* sorry. That's not funny. Really. I apologize."

I nodded. "I get it. Honest. And yeah, while the fact that he *died* is definitely not funny, I'm well aware that the 'how' he died is more than a little rib tickling. I have to admit I start chuckling when I imagine Darren with the bird mix in one hand, camera in the other, pencil behind his ear, and a parrot sleeping on his shoulder."

My eyes misted again but I smiled up at the fire fighter. "Darren was a good soul with a fantastic sense of humor. He was undoubtedly entertaining St. Peter himself with a few good jokes the instant he met him at the pearly gates. Probably dirty ones." I glanced up at Mark. "Darren was quite a bit older than I. He was my father's best friend. He married me after my dad died because Dad asked him to take care of me because it had just been him and me for years. And it seemed the right thing to do to get married. I did care about him. It's kind of fun now to envision Darren and my dad in heaven playing dominos and discussing the ramifications of sparrow feathers on the rain forests. Dad was another of those offbeat zoology professor types. And I'm sorry I'm rambling so much but right now it's the only thing between me and bloodcurdling screams."

Another spike hit. "Oh boy! I mean, *oh-ho-ho, boy!* Owie! Not fun, here."

"I wonder what's keeping your friend? It doesn't take that long to call 9-1-1."

A male voice answered the question. "*I'm* the hold up." I glanced behind Mark. The Marilyn Manson stripper held Ginny with one hand. The other held a gun. Big Bertha stood next to Ginny. Her hands had been tied behind her back with a bandana. "Hold-up" was right. Apparently our little birthing party was in the middle of one.

Surprisingly, the man with the weapon was the one who looked most distressed. He yelped, "I don't need this, ya know! I was just gonna take the money from the office and leave. But now—there's people. I don' know what to do. I don' wanna shoot nobody. Honest. What do I do?"

I glared at the wannabe robber. "*You* don't know what to do? *You* don't need this? What about me, you lousy little shit? I'm having a baby while some clown is robbing my daughter's birthplace. Oh, by the way, you have no rhythm. Good muscle tone. Lousy dancer. Come by my studio and we'll work on it in case you ever plan to sashay across a stage again."

Mark began to snicker. Bertha also bit back a smile. Ginny looked at me in horror. "Mimi! You just invited a criminal to take dance lessons. Are you nuts?"

"I'm not nuts. I'm in stinkin', severe damned awful pain! *Extreme* pain. I don't care if he takes every penny as long as he leaves and *Oh*, sweet Southern Comfort I don't know what I'm saying!"

I screamed. The burglar jumped about a foot in the air. Mark took advantage of this window of surprise and knocked the gun out of "Marilyn's'" hand and then kicked the kid to the floor. The robber didn't move for a second, and then he suddenly buried his face in his hands and began to cry. "I really didn't think anybody'd be here. Dammit. I *needed* this money."

"You stupid creep! *You* need money and you rob a place that was filled with unarmed women. And *we're* supposed to feel sorry for you? I'm bloody having a baby here, you toad! Try that sometime!" I spat.

He looked up with an expression of shock on his face. "You really are? I mean, right now? Wow. Ya know, I love kids. I got myself twelve nephews and nieces. I wanna have about ten some day. Oh my God. Is the baby really coming now?"

Four necks swiveled as one as we stared at him.

I gritted my teeth, "What the hell's it look like?"

"I blew it, didn't I?" He groaned.

Bertha snorted. "Pretty much. You moron. Why'd you think you could rob me and get away?"

Tears began to roll down the cheeks of the wannabe felon. Mark gently removed the gun from the spot where it had landed—a good six feet away from the kid. He stared at "Marilyn" and then growled, "Not a well-thought-out plan, kid."

The boy whimpered, "I thought it'd be a blast. Dance for all these hot girls, then grab some dough that only belonged to dogs. Get out before anybody even knew I'd done it."

Bertha growled. "*Only* belonged to dogs? You disgusting twerp. Where's that gun, Mark? Lemme at 'im."

The boy's eyebrows shot up to the top of his forehead. "Oh shoot. Didn' mean it. Nuthin's comin' out the way I want tonight. Honest, Miz Bertha, I like dogs. But I figgered it was money that wadden really owned by nobody. And if somebody saw me leave, she'd just think I didden take off my makeup. If they figured out it was me, they wouldn't really know because I gave Bertha a fake name."

The rank stupidity was astounding. But suddenly I didn't care. The time had come. Obviously, what I'd thought were the Braxton Hicks contractions earlier had been the "real" thing.

"Oh boy. Oh boy. *Oh boy, oh boy, oh boy!* Don't look now, but Baby is ready for a dramatic entrance."

I howled again and Ginny ran around the table. "Do you want to lie down? Start pushing? Whatever?"

"I am *not* lying down. I *was* going to have her in a nice birthing chair in the nice hospital with my nice doctor helping, while nice boring new age music played. But nooo! I'm in a flippin' bar, listening to disco tunes and arguing with an idiot burglar. No nice doctor. No sturdy birthing chair. So, you know what? I'm gonna get myself into a good ol' ballet second position *grande plié* and let 'er rip. For those of you not versed in ballet, that's a squat. A *big* damned squat."

Mark turned and tossed a set of keys toward Ginny. "I've got a first-aid kit in my car and a gym bag full of clean clothes. Grab 'em both, please. The red 'Vette in the parking lot. Clothes are in the trunk."

I gasped, "That's *your* 'Vette? It's so cool. I've always wanted . . .. *ow! Oooh! Ow!*" That morphed into "**&^%#!^!* and *&^%!@#!!*"

I pushed off the chair and arranged my body in the aforementioned big squat. Mark hunkered down to catch like he was behind home plate. And I began to experience undoubtedly the worst pain I'd ever endured which included a root canal, two torn ligaments, and a really spectacular appendix removal four years ago.

The sounds of disco pulsed through the club and penetrated my consciousness. *"Ladies Night."* Crap. That's what got me into this bar. *"Shake, Shake, Shake (Shake Your Booty.)"* Not great advice just now. Last up was Donna Summer's *"Love to Love You, Baby."* Well, whaddya know. Finally a song that made sense. I gave a last push during the final chorus.

A piercing cry rang out. Not mine. I looked down into Mark's hands and saw a beautiful, red face wrinkled in distress, and two blue eyes squinched but still staring up at me.

Mark proudly stated, "She's gorgeous."

"She is, isn't she? My daughter. This is too wonderful!"

Ginny had disappeared at some point during those last minutes and now returned with Mark's bag and white tablecloths soaked in water. "Bertha? Is it okay if we use these to clean her up?"

Bertha grinned. "It's fine, Hon. This is a first, y'all. A baby born at *Big Bertha's*. What's a linen or two? Hey! I just got a great idea. I'll host a shower for you. Could make the cover charge baby toys and diapers and those cute little onesies and formulas or whatever." She looked at me then with awe. "Dang! I gotta hand it to you, girl. You can let'em fly. You know cuss words I've never heard before!"

I smiled, sweetly. "Me? Cuss? Never."

Mark quit dealing with scissors and cords. "Shame. Fibbing in front of your child barely a minute after she's entered the world."

His expression was soft and lovely and my heart thudded. I'd fallen in love with two people in one night. Although, to be accurate, I'd fallen for my child eight-and-a-half months ago. But time didn't matter. Feelings and people did.

Mark placed my little girl in my arms and gazed at her with amazement and adoration.

We'd all forgotten our inept robber. He looked at my baby, stupefied. "Whoa. It's like— a real live kid. Awesome, dude!"

Bertha sighed. "Honey, you're one lousy thief. Your vocabulary and grammar stink. You're a crummy stripper. But seeing that look in your eyes makes me think you might just make a decent father one day. Now untie my hands before I kick you senseless, you little twit."

He did so, looking like a stray dog waiting in the pouring rain for someone to come rescue him. "I guess I go to jail, now?"

Bertha looked at Mark, Ginny, and me with raised eyebrows. "Nobody got hurt, you didn't try and go for the gun after Mark knocked it away, you didn't actually get any money, and you know you did wrong. I'll cut you a break if you'll come by and wash dishes for me for the next six months— you goony kid."

Mark shrugged. "Forgive and forget." His expression hardened. "But if I find out you're engaging in any more criminal activity including getting a single parking ticket, I'll personally tattoo that awful makeup onto your face for life."

The goony kid hugged everyone but me. I wasn't in the mood and I made my position clear. He plopped back down and began wiping off his make-up. Without the paint, he couldn't have been more than eighteen—if that. I wondered if he was even old enough to be in *Bertha's*. The thought made me chuckle as I cradled my daughter. "Hey, she's not legal in here, is she? Wouldn't you know it. My first time in a strip joint and I'm sharing it with my underage daughter."

Mark maneuvered himself so he could hold me while I held my baby. Sister Sledge's *"We Are Family"* played over the speakers.

Ginny asked, "What are you going to name her? We've been calling her Mini-Mimi, but I know that's not exactly what you want."

I glanced at Mark. "Well, I've been thinking while everyone was dealing with our wanna be bar-robber. And what keeps hitting me is the name Donna. In honor of a certain dancer's routine to a great Donna Summer song, and his subsequent incredibly fabulous aid to one tiny ballerina in labor. Let's say this is a six-pound token of my appreciation?"

The ladies and the burglar nodded with enthusiasm. Mark's eyes misted a bit. "Thanks." He smiled at me and chuckled. "Hopefully, the next time I see you and Donna, it will be in less stressful circumstances.

I nodded. "Miss Donna says a big 'yes.' And so does her Mama Mimi." I tentatively added, "Tell you what. I'll cook you a big batch of tamales, okay?" I twisted slightly to turn and look up into those dark eyes.

Mark smiled down at me. "You're on."

Ginny chortled, *"Great!* Sandra and I got something right today. You finally have that same expression you did when you won the trip to Paris. So, the Labor Day mommy napping was okay even if the cosmetics didn't exactly last the night?"

I grinned. "You nailed it. I *am* experiencing pure joy. Thanks one and all for one whale of a great ladies night."

END

Wilkinson Roses

Four o'clock. I had about an hour before the sand-and-surf covered college kids headed for the bar next door to indulge in the two-for-one margaritas and began wandering into my store. It should be enough time to dig through the boxes of "whatever" I'd purchased Saturday in Houston for three hundred dollars. No one, including the auctioneer, had had a clue as to what Miss Bessie Anne Tatum had stuffed inside them for the past eighty-five years. I hoped for treasure, but feared I'd find trash.

I shut the front door of *Legends,* and then headed for the storeroom, where I'd stacked the boxes from the estate sale. I ripped open carton number one, and was thrilled to discover items that had once stood on a dresser, including a small jewelry box (empty), an infuser bottle still maintaining the perfume scents from seventy or more years ago, and the unbroken hand-held mirror. I snuck a peek at myself to see if I needed to do any repair work on my own make-up and hair and was relieved to see the mascara still intact and my brunette, newly-cut bob unfazed by the Galveston humidity.

I put the vanity items back into the carton, and then opened the second box, almost shouting in sheer glee when I saw the first piece of a set of very old, very exquisite china.

I picked up a cup, cream-colored, holding one perfectly formed red rose dead center, so real and so sharply defined I almost expected the tiny thorns to prick my finger.

I gently placed the cup down on the quilt I'd spread out on the floor, and then lifted out the rest of the china, until I was surrounded by cream and roses. Not a chip or a scratch marred the surface of any piece. Even the teapot was unstained.

It was fairly obvious Miss Bessie had never used these dishes. They were so pristine it appeared doubtful *anyone* had ever used these dishes in the last hundred years. For one wild, impractical moment I considered keeping them for myself. Serving tea to someone who appreciated fine china. Someone who appreciated fine conversation. Someone who appreciated . . . me.

I sighed, letting the vision evaporate. I *sell* antiques and items that are still too new to be considered antiques. I don't own them. "Gemma, you're a dimwit. Do not go there. This china could be your ticket for putting *Legends* into the black. Really, one good buyer for a set like this would do it."

I held a plate up to the light and nearly dropped it. A figure was reflected in the dish. Not good. I'd left my baseball bat under the front counter. Right next to my cell phone with the big buttons that so easily read 9-1-1.

I swallowed, and then called out, "Is someone there? Didn't you see the 'closed 'til five' sign?"

The reflection became a shadow. Appeared male. If he'd seen that sign, he'd ignored it. Rude, illiterate, or dangerous. Take your pick. If I had my druthers I'd go with illiterate.

He murmured what sounded like, "I've found her."

I turned and blinked in disbelief. He was dressed in a white linen long shirt, topped by a deep tan leather longer jacket, and brown pants that appeared to be some kind of wool blend (ridiculous for Galveston weather even in early April) with a brown scarf tied loosely at his neck and matching brown leather knee-high boots. A wide-brimmed brown hat topped long, dark brown hair tied back in a ponytail. Talk about retro. I hadn't seen his face but the overall effect was intensely male.

Then it hit me. The only possibility that made sense. "Excuse me, but are you one of the actors rehearsing the movie about the Texas Revolution downtown. Let's see. Uh. Sam Houston? Daniel Bowie? Davy Crockett? Can't be Crockett—no coonskin cap, unless the old Disney show's costume department was way off base. Whatever. Look, I don't want to be inhospitable but I'm closed until five." *(And how did you get in here through the locked door, anyway?)*

His next step brought him into the light where I finally saw his face. Firm chin, straight nose, and warm hazel eyes a shade lighter than his hair. I gazed at him, finding it hard to breathe. Could one fall in love at first sight of a burglar?

He smiled at me, and then gestured down toward the china before softly saying, "Wilkinson Roses."

"What?"

"The set is called Wilkinson Roses. Eighteen-fifties. Do you like the dishware?"

An actor who knew about china patterns and wanted to discuss his knowledge? Interesting. I wondered, suddenly, crazily, if he enjoyed tea.

I tentatively nodded. "Like? That's putting it mildly. Make that I *love* this set. But it's odd. I've studied hundreds of books about antiques. I've visited exhibits and museums and antique stores every chance I've had since I was a little kid, but I've honestly never seen a pattern like this. It's beyond beautiful. It's unequaled. Do you mind if I ask how you know the name? Are you related to Miss Bessie?" I felt a pain under my ribs. I hurriedly asked, "Do you . . . want them back? Do you think I cheated you on the price? It was fair. *Really.* I might have ended up with a bunch of plastic forks or something for all anyone knew since the cartons were sealed."

He shook his head. "You didn't cheat me and I'm not here to take them."

"Okay. Why *are* you here, then? And *who* are you? If you're here to cause trouble, I really don't need more on my plate. I've had enough for a lifetime. My parents are dead. I owe every creditor in Texas thanks to taking a huge risk and opening the store eight months ago. I dated a creep last year who mistook me for a punching bag. I slugged him back, filed charges and left Dallas for Galveston as fast as I could. Which reminds me, I have a baseball bat and I'm not afraid to swing it."

Good grief. Where had that come from? I was spilling my guts to a stranger while simultaneously threatening him with bodily harm, which was somewhat impossible to follow through on, since the door to the storeroom and the shop's counter were between the Louisville slugger and me.

He frowned. "You are too refined, genteel and kind a lady to use a weapon. I'm sorry if I frightened you, and I'm devastated to hear sorry your life hasn't been pleasant. Such wrongs should be set right. You seem to believe I'm a thief here to steal your treasures, and I want to reassure you I have no such intention. The only treasure I need is a moment of your time. Will you give it?"

"Oh. Sure. Why not?" Heck. I could listen . . . or do a Mickey Mantle with the bat if I ooched toward the shop door, put on a little speed, and dove behind the counter before he knew what I was doing. I preferred listening.

He abruptly asked, "I'm curious. What are those bronze items on your desk?"

"You mean the ugly bunnies keeping my reference books from tumbling everywhere?"

"Ah, yes. Bookends. Of course. But they appear to represent dogs, rather than hares."

"Well, I got them at a yard sale for fifty cents. They seem comfortable back here, but you might be right about the species. Dogs. Possible." I smiled. "Just no breed I've ever seen."

His tone grew wistful. "I once owned a pair of collies. They were beautiful, intelligent creatures. I had great affection for them."

"I love dogs, too. If I can ever get my landlord to fix the fence in my yard, I want to adopt a couple from the local pound."

He appeared confused. "Pound?"

"Shelter? As in strays and puppies?"

"I don't know about such places."

Now I was confused. "Where've you been hiding? Gilligan's Island?"

"Where is that?"

Terrific. I was dealing with a lunatic or an agoraphobic who'd been holed up in a cave watching 1950s era Westerns for far too long. A stunningly handsome lunatic but . . . well, either way I needed to hear what this was all about. "Forget it. You said you wanted a moment of my time? It's yours. Talk."

"Thank you." He paused, before stating, "I made the Wilkinson Roses for my mother. As a gift."

I was confused. "Wait. So you're claiming these are *not* antiques? Sorry, but I don't believe you. I'm good at my trade. These pieces are clearly more than a hundred years old. Closer to a hundred and fifty."

"I didn't say they weren't old. You're quite correct in your assessment as to their age. But I swear to you I made this set, which I named after my mother's family, the Wilkinsons. I am a Baldridge. Mr. Joshua Baldridge."

I blinked. Either my hearing was going, the man really *was* a total nutter, or Mr. Baldridge had found the secret of youth since he appeared to be no more than thirty. Fine. I'd play along. "Nice to meet you. I'm Gemma Harrison. Owner of *Legends* here. New owner of the very antique Wilkinson Roses. And a woman who would love to know why you're claiming you crafted china made more than a hundred years ago."

He closed his eyes. "What year is this?"

I exhaled. "Twenty-fifteen. *Damn.* Here it comes, right? The sting. You're going to tell me you time-traveled here. From Eighteen-forty-eight or something. Right? Super." I felt like crying. "Is this some new reality show? Actors dressed like they've been at the Alamo all day pop in on shop owners and make them look like total bozos? Where's the camera? Do I have time to run a comb through my hair and smear on a little lip gloss?"

"I have no idea what you're talking about." He perked up like a kid a Christmas. "You mentioned time travel? Is it possible now? What a marvel of advanced invention!"

"*Enough!*" I exhaled." Look, just go back to your buddies on the set and get the video up online. Let it go viral and have the world see what a kick it was to make a fool of me."

Joshua Baldridge appeared stricken. "I am very sorry, Miss Harrison, if I've done something to offend you. Believe me, that is not my intention."

"What exactly *is* your intention?"

He didn't answer right away. A myriad of possibilities, all of them deliciously romantic, and some purty danged wicked, began flooding my brain.

Then he smiled. "Honorable, Miss Harrison. Although, I'm afraid you will find my intentions absurd, perhaps insanely so. However, while your mind and your practical brain might not believe me, I somehow feel certain that your heart and your soul will listen."

I raised an eyebrow. "Mr. Baldridge? Go ahead and shell out whatever b.s. you're selling before I throw the bookends at you."

"B.S.?"

"Skip it. Tell me all about making Nineteenth Century dishware."

He gestured toward the teapot, and a look of sadness crossed his beautiful features. "That was my favorite piece. It still is." He paused, and then stared into my eyes. "My family and I moved to Texas in Eighteen-forty from New York. My father was in the business of shipping and Galveston, as the capital of the Republic of Texas, was a thriving city. I joined my father's company when I was fifteen, but always loved making beautiful pieces." He smiled. "I suppose it was my way of pretending I was an artist, which was a profession frowned upon by my father. Now, Miss Gemma, you may think this to be fantastic, but I designed and crafted the Wilkinson Roses in Eighteen-fifty, when I was twenty years old. Mama was unable to ever use the set, as she passed away only a month after I presented her with the china. She told me before she died that it was her wish the set would be a gift to the lady I took as my bride."

He'd nailed it. Fantastic.

"Look, that sounds interesting, as well as a bit frustrating, and sad about your mom, but what you're telling me is also impossible."

"Would you indulge me in a favor?"

"What?"

He pointed to the teapot. "Please, reach inside. You will find more than air. The explanation. But you need to see the words first."

What the heck. I figured there were no snakes curled up inside, so I shouldn't be bitten and die before I opened the shop in the next few minutes. I reached around and discovered a scrap of parchment, pulled it out, unrolled it, and read aloud the ink-stained poetry.

Only after the last petal falls, shall love live.

"That's lovely," I said. I looked into Joshua's hazel eyes. "I assume you know what it means?"

The bell jangled from outside *Legends*. Damn. "Joshua. Uh. Mr. Baldridge. It's five. I've got to reopen. I'm sorry."

"Miss Harrison, please wait."

I paused in the doorway between the storeroom and the shop. "I have to go. I can't afford to lose any sales."

He quickly stated, "I beg you, please listen. If the Wilkinson Roses are not shattered within the next twenty-four hours, I will vanish until the next owner claims them."

"What? What the hell are you saying?"

He closed his eyes for a moment, then opened them and stared at me. "I am cursed. God help me, but it's true. I carry with me a curse that can only be cured through love." He lowered his volume. "*Your* love, Gemma. You must already think I'm insane so it doesn't matter if I also tell you that soon as I met you, I knew if I wasn't able to stay with *you* and no one else, I felt it wouldn't matter if I vanished forever."

Wow. A sandwich short of a picnic. A spark plug short of . . . well whatever spark plugs become when they get together. He was handsome, and intelligent . . . and loco. I didn't know whether I should be calling a cop, a shrink, a shaman, a medium or all the above. I closed my eyes for a second trying to decide what to do.

When I opened them, he was gone. Vanished. The window was locked, the exit to the back of the storeroom closed and bolted. It was mid-April in Galveston, Texas but I was freezing.

The doorbell jangled again, followed by someone pounding on the door.

I plastered a fake smile on my face and hurried back into the shop and unlocked the front door, which didn't help give me any answers as to how Joshua Baldridge had managed to enter the place about forty minutes earlier. I stayed busy with customers for the next four hours. I'd been keeping *Legends* open until 10:30 through Spring Break, but this night I closed at nine. I couldn't take the noise somehow. I couldn't stand answering questions about Nineteenth Century music boxes or the beautiful lacework on tablecloths asked by often inebriated customers too young to understand the history behind those items.

I padlocked the front door and headed down the street to the bungalow I rented, which was close to the beach. But I didn't stop. I kept walking toward the pier, ignoring the tourists still gleefully frolicking in the Gulf waters, until I reached the end of the ramp and simply stood looking out over the water. I turned around and started back home when I realized I couldn't stop envisioning Nineteenth Century ships coming to the port with their wares and their immigrants. Which led me to dreaming about a man dressed in the clothes of that era sitting down and crafting a set of rose-patterned dishes.

I opened *Legends* at nine the next morning. I should have been grateful for the non-stop stream of eager buyers. Instead I was irritated. I hadn't had a chance to check the storeroom at all. To check the china. To look for Joshua Baldridge.

Four o'clock. Finally. Early dinner break time. I locked the front door, flipped the sign to read, *Closed 'til 5:00*, and then headed back to the storage area.

There was no one in sight. I was absurdly disappointed. What had I expected? That Joshua Baldridge would be sitting cross-legged on the quilt between a platter and a gravy bowl, stirring tea into an exquisite saucer, reciting poetry and waiting for Gemma Harrison to come dispel some wacky fairy-tale curse?

"Shoot. Talk about cuckoo city, Gemma. Just dive in and join the Thorazine and straight-jacket crowd, why don't you?"

"I would hate for you to join any crowed, Miss Harrison, that sounds so unpleasant."

I whirled around. "Joshua? How did you get inside? I padlocked that door."

He didn't answer. We stood and stared at each other. It didn't matter how he'd gotten inside the storeroom He was here.

"Miss Gemma. We were interrupted last evening and much as I would like to share a cup of tea with you and discuss the affairs of the day, I *must* tell you now. You must hear this before the clock strikes five."

Uh oh. We'd hauled in the old *before the clock hits the hour . . .* bit. I didn't care. He was here. He was great to look at. My heart hadn't raced like this since the last marathon I ran about five years ago when I'd been on the college track team. "Fine. Go ahead. Regale me with tales of weirdness."

He grinned, although there was a trace of near panic in his eyes. "I'll endeavor to be brief. Miss Gemma, I am . . . that is . . . I was . . . a wealthy man with a large inheritance. In Eighteen-fifty-six, I was a man preparing to choose a bride with whom to share that wealth." He shook his head. "The list of eligible Texas debutantes included Miss Charity Devere."

"Oh-kay. Charity Devere. Smacks of celebrity somehow. Or a really cool drag queen. Oops, sorry. I'm interrupting and not making sense. Go on. Charity. Nice name. Another word for kindness, altruism and love."

"Sadly, Miss Devere's character did not match her name. I hate to speak ill of any woman, but she was greedy, unkind, possessed of a shrill voice, a shrewish attitude, and a mother who was very displeased that I had clearly let it be known I had not the slightest wish to ask for Charity's hand in marriage." He added, "I allowed my distaste to overtake my manners. I informed Charity's mother that her daughter needed lessons in comportment and the art of speaking since her voice often imitated the cry of the sea gulls that sweep to shore in search of unwary fish. I then expressed sympathy with the fish."

I couldn't help but laugh. It was a neat story so far, even if the players had been dead for more than a hundred years. I shied away from that thought. Too outlandish to contemplate. "Sorry. I can just imagine hearing the sounds of Charity and her mom flapping their beaks. Go on."

He smiled. "I share some of your amusement. To this day I fail to understand how I could have been ensnared in the web of madness surrounding mother and daughter. Mrs. Devere claimed that I would eternally regret shaming Charity. I ignored her vile threats until the evening she paid me a visit bringing with her an ancient woman from New Orleans who claimed to be a voodoo princess."

"Oh boy. I see this coming a mile away. Diss the daughter and whammo! Enter the Big Curse. Call the National Enquirer now."

Joshua stared at me. "I beg your pardon?"

"You really don't . . .? Never mind. I shouldn't have said that. And truly, I'm enchanted." I paused before adding "But then, so are *you*, right?"

"I'm well aware of how this sounds. I am. Curses? The stuff of childish nightmares and stories whispered in the night. Yet my own nightmare began when I met the woman who called herself Queen Rada Loa more than hundred years ago, if the date you gave me last evening is correct."

"Check the calendar over the counter if you don't believe me." I reached into my pocket. "Or here. Cell phone. Date, time, and Internet access."

"I'll take you at your word." He smiled. "Miss Gemma, won't you please consider taking me at mine?"

When he smiled like that I considered taking his word, his body, and his heart on a long cruise around the world. An entire century with him would be fine. I never imagined such a formal use of my name would make me want to feel the user's lips on mine, feel his hands roaming through my hair, feel . . .

I inhaled. "Continue. I'll be quiet and try to keep an open mind."

"Thank you. So, Mrs. Devere introduced me to Queen Rada Loa, who spent a few moments staring at the belongings in the dining room, which included a china cabinet holding the Wilkinson Rose set. She smiled, oddly, scribbled something on parchment and gave it to me. The exact paper you read last night. She informed me that I was doomed to vanish and materialize only when the Wilkinson Roses appeared. I was doomed to explain the circumstances of the curse and the china, no matter who owned the set at a specific time. My feelings toward the woman did not matter. If a lady loved me enough to be willing to destroy the china, my curse would end. I remember a second smile, almost sincere in nature, claiming the curse *could* even become a blessing one day. But, only when the last dish was shattered would I be allowed to come back to life and love."

For a fairy tale, I thought it was pretty original. Spooky but oddly charming. I didn't remember anything even in the Brothers Grimm repertoire that mentioned smashing china services to destroy curses imposed by bitchy voodoo queens.

"Joshua. Assuming I buy any of this, how many times have you, uh, come back?"

"Three. The last time I appeared was in Nineteen-fifty-two when Miss Tatum received the Wilkinson Roses."

"Wait. You mean Bessie?"

"Yes. Elizabeth Anne Tatum. She bought the dishes in a store in Dallas if my recollections are correct. She declined to destroy the china. She was far more interested in wealth than in love. She *did* believe that particular aspect of the curse."

"Whoa. Hang on there. What are you talking about? What does wanting to be rich have to do with this?"

"If the china remains intact, I disappear until a new owner takes possession. In the meanwhile, the owner of the intact china gains wealth beyond compare."

"Yow." I tried to take all this in. When I spoke again, my question surprise me. "Did you love her?"

"Who?"

"Bessie. Elizabeth Tatum."

"No. To be honest, I was relieved to know I would not be spending my life with her. Disappearing for another fifty years or more seemed preferable. Bessie Tatum had many characteristics similar to Charity Devere."

I had to ask. "Did *she* love you?"

He shook his head. "No. She claimed to, in the time we spent together. But as you see, the china is intact. I have no idea what her true feelings were."

"And mine?" Damn. I hadn't meant to blurt that out.

His voice became soft, low, and innocently seductive. "You know the answer, Gemma."

I did. I walked over to him and touched his arm. I screamed when my hand dove clear through.

"Oh dear God! You're not real! You *are* a ghost! Or I'm hallucinating."

I stared at him, desperate to touch his flesh, and terrified that I'd lost my sanity. Perhaps I'd been so unhappy after my last disastrous relationship I'd imagined the perfect, yet unattainable, man? Here was a way to dream about someone without getting hurt. At least physically. Emotionally was another story.

Joshua looked directly into my eyes. "Gemma, I have very little time left. And if you believe nothing else I've said, please know this. If I had been given the choice of the woman who would receive the Wilkinson Roses, I would have chosen no other than you. My story is crazy, and perhaps so is loving someone the instant one gazes into soft blue eyes, yet I met you and I fell in love with your wit and your sweetness and your laughter and your willingness to listen. I love the way your eyes show me every thought and feeling you have. It may be madness, but I love you."

The doorbell at the front of the shop started jangling. I glanced toward the entrance and shouted, "Still closed!"

When I turned back around, Joshua, again, had vanished.

I held up my cell phone and looked at the glowing clock on the front of small tablet. Ten minutes until five. I picked up the clock on my desk. Same thing. Not even an extra minute to think.

The parchment lay next to the desk clock. *Only after the last petal falls, shall love live.*

Joshua's words echoed inside my mind. "It may be madness, but I love you."

I had no time to decide whether this all was one big hoax. No time to debate the truth of the fable told by a ghost. No time to consider the risk I was about to take, knowing my actions could bring the loss of my shop.

I picked up the gravy bowl, exhaled, and then threw it against the brick walls of the storeroom. The soup tureen and the meat platter followed. I grabbed pieces and threw them like a baseball pitcher on crack. The teapot was the last to go.

The clock chimed five. I stood amidst the wreckage, waiting and praying for Joshua to appear.

All remained quiet. My clever, magical ghost was doubtless down at the *Two-Step* bar hoisting a few pints along and regaling his fellow actors with how he'd hoodwinked an antiques dealer into destroying her business, not to mention any chance of ever trusting another human being in her life.

I didn't bother to open up. I left by the back exit, locked the door, and walked home. And cried.

I was back at *Legends* at eight in the morning, preparing to calculate what I needed to sell to make next month's rent. Hell, I didn't even have the three hundred dollars I'd spent buying the Wilkinson Roses. It lay in pieces in a back room I didn't want to see for the next ten years or so. I sat behind the counter and slowly began to look through my accounts.

The front doorbell jangled. It was too early for customers. I walked to the door, opened it and stared into hazel eyes just a shade lighter than the dark brown hair framing a handsome face.

"Joshua?"

He grinned. "In the flesh."

He leaned down. Our lips met. I could feel the warmth and the solid, honest presence, which was also damned sexy. We kissed and held each other until I worried the locals would come pouring out of the diner next door, forgetting breakfast and each one bearing a giant marker with which to smear "Adult Entertainment Only" all over *Legends'* windows.

I pulled Joshua inside. "I am . . . I don't know what to say. I barely know what to feel." I winced. "And I hate to bring this up following what have been the nicest and most romantic moments in my life, but I suppose we should head to the storeroom and check the damage. I've been avoiding it. How the heck am I going to explain two hundred shattered pieces or more of dishes to my insurance company? Sorry to be so practical but it was a major mess last night when I left."

"Gemma, trust me. You won't need to contact anyone."

We walked hand in hand to the back. I stopped in the doorway, stunned. Every piece of the Wilkinson Roses lay in perfect condition on the quilt on the floor. Undamaged. Not even a tiny scratch on the teapot.

I fell back into Joshua's strong arms. "I don't understand. I smashed them. I mean, they were powder."

"I wasn't allowed to tell you. It had to be your choice. Love or wealth. You had to love me enough to be willing to destroy the china." Joshua picked up the teapot that had held the parchment. He smiled. "I can finally hold this—and you." The smile broadened. "Tea?"

"Yes, but in a bit. I need a little more information, Mr. Baldridge, or I'm going to need something a lot stronger than tea."

"I'm sorry. Queen Rada Loa claimed if I loved and was loved in return, the broken pieces would become whole again. I had no idea if she was lying or not until I saw the dishes in here—intact."

I turned on the hot plate I kept in the storeroom, grabbed a tin of tea from a shelf by the exit door, and shook the leaves into an antique strainer. Once the water was hot, I poured the tea into the undamaged cups.

We sat on the quilt, surrounded by beauty created by Joshua a hundred and fifty-odd years earlier.

I was still in shock but excited and happier than I ever remembered feeling my entire life. "I never imagined when I named my shop *Legends*, I'd be a living one."

Joshua winked. "A toast? How about to Queen Rada Loa, who cursed me, yet still found a way to bring love into my life?"

"Sounds good. Oh! And to Bessie Tatum. For being too greedy to choose love over treasures. Poor deluded woman."

We lifted our cups and gently tapped them against each other, watching as the red roses touched.

Joshua softly said, "To legends that come true. And to love that lasts forever."

END

CENTER FLOOR

Jesse and I would sharpen our dancing skills at my house after school. Shoes off, records on, rugs rolled up, we'd hear opening chords and head straight for center floor. We'd attract an admiring crowd of two—my mom and the family dog, Princess. We were very good.

Jesse stood four inches taller than my 5'4", perfect for spinning me in under-arm turns. Latin heritage was evident in his wavy, black hair, brown eyes, and toffee colored complexion. He had full lips, a flat nose, and enviably high cheekbones.
I described myself as early German/Irish peasant. Fair skin, long strawberry blonde hair, hazel eyes, and a too-thin face. Both of us had been blessed with rhythm, grace, and far too much energy.

The dances after football games became our performing venues. Jesse would wait for me to change out of my majorette costume, then we'd run together towards the local band (Usually *The Morticians*.)
"Hi! Could ya'll please play . . .?"
"*Gloria*, right? Van Morrison? We know, we know."
Gloria was our favorite dance song. Every note, every beat and every cymbal crash was imbedded in our muscle memory.

Hearing the opening chords, we'd head straight for center floor. We always attracted a crowd. We were very good.

Jesse signed my yearbook "friends forever", and that's what we remained. We didn't date each other. We commiserated with each other. Jesse was madly in love with my best friend, Cynthia. I was madly in love with Grady. Florence to Jesse late night phone chats were routine.

"Jesse? Word isn't out yet, but I wanted you to know. Leonard just broke up with Cynthia."

"Oh my gosh. Is she okay?"

Pause.

"Jesse, you're too nice to be real. Cynthia is my best friend and I've spent hours letting her cry on my shoulder. You're nuts about her and you're supposed to have ulterior motives and ask if there's any way she'll fall for you."

"I'm not stupid. She and I will never be more than good friends. I will forever cherish her in unrequited love."

"You've been reading bad Gothic novels again, haven't you?"

"Well, yes."

"Forget this romantic suffering hero stuff. Ask her out!"

Or:

"Florence! Florence!"

"What?"

"Remember this afternoon when you were sitting in the bleachers watching basketball practice and Steve came over the rail and started chasing you?"

I smiled wickedly. "Oh, uh ...yes."

"Well, Grady was watching the whole time. He threw the basketball into the corner and stalked off into the locker room."

"Good. I hope he's jealous. By the way, Steve and I are going out after Friday's game."

Regardless of our romantic misadventures, Jesse and I ended up spending more time together than couples officially going steady. When we weren't dancing at my house or involved in school activities, we'd drive around town together.

We'd browse through record stores checking out the latest hits from England. We'd go shopping and look for the latest styles from England. We'd grab a pizza at *Giovanni's*, and ask the guitarist to play the latest hits from England while we tried to figure out where to get enough money to *buy* the latest styles from England.

One afternoon over a pepperoni and mushroom, we heard that Bucky was in the middle of a burger-stuffing challenge with Randy at What-a-Burger and drove over to cheer them on.

"Slam dunk, Miss Florence. Randy outweighs Bucky by 100 pounds."

"Ah, but Bucky is smarter. He'll have a strategy. You just watch."

Crammed into a booth meant for four people were six classmates. Jesse and I slid next to them.

"Go, Randy!" Marty, Randy's girl, was screaming in full cheerleader voice.

"Buck-ee! Buck-EE! BUCK-EE!"

The chanting grew louder from Cynthia, Connie, and Steve.

I joined in with:

"Bucky, Bucky, he's our man

He'll eat more than Bubba can!"

Jesse stared at me.

"That was terrible."

I shrugged. "You want good poetry, read Emily Dickinson or Shakespeare. This is a heated moment in sports history."

A heated moment that ended when a green-faced Randy lunged for the restroom while Bucky grinned, and then calmly and slowly finished his pile of burgers.

I never drove Jesse home. He wouldn't allow it. He lived with his grandmother in a part of town known as No Man's Land. None of the surrounding cities claimed the area, leaving its residents with dirt roads, no police or fire department, and little sanitation.

Jesse was silent on the subject of where and how he lived. I knew certain facts. I knew No Man's Land was not a safe place. I knew Jesse had family besides Grandmother, somewhere. I knew he'd been given a scholarship based on low economic level from St. Francis Parish to attend our high school.

I never pressed Jesse for further details. His privacy and his feelings were more important. Besides, we had more important, weighty topics to discuss.

"I want to develop this with a matte finish. It evokes a much softer emotion."

"Emotion, schmotion! I'm not looking for emotion, Jesse. I want a publicity photo for the recital. Professional headshots are always glossy 8 X 10's."

"So, when you become a professional dancer, you'll get glossy. Right now, you get matte."

I got matte.

And:

"I went to the Peter, Paul & Mary concert. My brothers took me, so Mom said I could stay out later. It was great. We got to talk to them after. They were so nice. Bob and I talked to Paul and Don was discussing guitars with Peter."

"That's too cool. Hey, did you know Grady stayed up all night to get tickets?"

I sniffed. "He told me. Mind you, he didn't ask me to go with him. He went with some group from the college. I thought it was funny. If he'd gone with us, he could've stayed and met Peter and Paul. As it turned out, he had to leave 'cause the cute little sorority girls had curfew. They were in by even when the concert was still going on. That'll teach him. Fink."

Talking about Peter, Paul and Mary invariably led to us singing folk and protest songs. We knew the words to Bob Dylan's *Subterranean Homesick Blues*, and could harmonize through Simon & Garfunkel's *The Sounds of Silence*. We were even able to sing the anti-war counterpoint Canticle in *Scarborough Fair*. We were very good.

We loved to sing. We put our gifts to use in the Glee Club. Jesse was a gifted singer with a pure, perfectly pitched voice and an incredible range. He rightfully had his share of solos. He could sing tenor. He could sing bass.

I had a good range, good pitch, and could read music. I moved from soprano to alto sections, as needed. Jesse and I held the Glee Club together. The director, Sister Clara Francis, doubtless thought differently, but was too polite to say so.

As mobile vocalists, Jesse and I would be placed side by side during practice – a potentially disruptive situation. We loved to sing. We also loved to talk. We did both.

"Pssst."

"What?"

"They're putting my artwork up at the fair."

"Jesse, that's soooo cool."

"They might even put prices on some of the paintings."

"Wow! "

"Florence Ann, *Be Quiet*!"

"Sorry, Sister, but Jesse was just . . .

"Don't 'but Jesse was just' me. I saw *you* talking. We have too much work to do and as usual, you're disrupting the group."

"Sorry, Sister."

"Sister?"

"Yes, Jesse?"

"It's my fault. I was telling Florence about my artwork getting put up at the fair this weekend."

This pronouncement would be followed by one of Jesse's delightfully infectious giggles.

Followed by Sister exclaiming, "*Oh! Jesse*, that's wonderful! Choir, everyone needs to go to the fair and see Jesse's work."

I'd sigh and shake my head.

Jesse's giggle could equally charm singing nuns or delight screaming children. He and I taught catechism classes in a tiny, Hispanic, farming community where Jesse became the kids' hero. In Spanish, he'd tell stories not necessarily authorized by the Vatican. Gleeful shrieks would be erupting from his young audience down the hall from where I tried, without success, to keep my kids focused.

"Jesse, what are you teaching them?"

"Oh … just the parable of the prodigal son."

"I don't remember that parable as being a real side splitter. Are you adding something?"

This query would be acknowledged with a sweet smile. (Jesse had the sweetest smile of any creature on God's earth.) I also knew behind the smile lurked funny thoughts.

I imagine if questioned today, those pupils might not recall specific church dogma. But they'd remember the laughter.

Jesse could laugh at himself as easily as he could make others laugh around him. About a week before graduation, he and I decided to visit the zoo. Jesse used up a roll of film that day, posing me saluting with bald eagles, preening with peacocks, balancing with ostriches.

Mid-afternoon, I pulled a Dr. Doolittle. A llama was eyeing us across its small pasture.

"Here, llama, llama, llama. Come model for us. Come here, girl, come on, baby, there's a good llama."

Trotting over, it stuck its nose in my hand, and whinnied.

I patted it on its head.

"Nice llama. Can you smile for Jesse's camera?"

Teeth bared, it snorted fiercely at Jesse.

"It's going to bite me! I can tell she hates me! For that matter, how do you know it's a she?"

"She's got a pink collar on. And she doesn't hate you. You're just being a wimp. Besides, she's on the other side of the fence. Come pat her and take the picture!"

"Look at those teeth. I'm going to be ripped to shreds! I'm staying as far away as I can."

He took the shot—fast—then took off running. Faster.

I found him by the monkey cage. We stared at each other. Then the laughter exploded, bringing with it streaming tears, and aching sides.

We had much the same reaction when we saw the photos. For some reason, the llama and I are flashing similar smiles.

After high school, Jesse and I gradually saw less of each other. We'd go to an occasional rock concert together. And, of course, we'd call late at night.

"I'm madly in love with Sid."

"Wait, weren't you madly in love with Greg last week?"

"That was *last* week. Jeez, Jesse, keep up with the calendar."

"I'm trying but I think your love life is getting too confusing. " Pause. "Hey, did you see Cynthia this week?"

"Yeah, I did. Guess what? She's using her real name now. Did you know it's Hyacinth? She decided it had more flower power.

Are you still nuts about her?

"Well, (long pause) "I still like to hear what she's up to. Um . . . I met a girl at church a couple of weeks ago. She's really nice and really pretty. Her name is Elicia."

"Well, Hallelujah and Praise the Lord! Have you asked her out yet?"

"Give me time."

"Jesse, I adore you, but you are a mess."

We attended Elicia's wedding (to Rafael) and the baptism of her child a couple of years later.

One Christmas during college, Jesse and I sang for a candlelight peace rally. Our voices were in harmony; our sentiments were in unison. It was our last singing performance together.

At our twentieth high school reunion, Jesse and I met again. He was working and couldn't stay long. But then we heard the opening chords and headed straight for center floor. We still attracted a crowd. We were still very good.

Mom sent me the obituary notice.

Name. Age.

Died this day…

Funeral mass, burial, survived by a son, brother, nieces and
nephews.
Sang with the choir at St. Francis.
Jesse had a son.
I never knew.

Died this day…

I still sharpen my dancing skills at home. Shoes off, CDs on, rugs
rolled back, I hear opening chords and head straight for center
floor.

Jesse's there. We attract a crowd. We're very good.

In loving memory of Jesse Castanon . . . "friends forever."

About the Author:

Flo Fitzpatrick was born in Washington, D.C. and spent her first years traveling across oceans and countries as an Army brat. She has very little memory of living in a chateau outside of Orléans, France but is certain the Gothic nature of the castle inspired her to write. After earning degrees in dance and theatre Flo shuttled from Texas to New York City, performing, choreographing and teaching. She still loves both states for their ability to spawn wacky and diverse characters who tweak her writer's imagination. Flo's website is www.flofitzpatrick.com

Mystery/ Romance/ Paranormal
Ghosts, Wandering Here and There (formerly Ghost of a Chance)
It's a Marvelous Night for a Moondance
Haunting Melody

Abby Fouchet Mysteries:
Blackout Over Broadway (formerly Sweet Dreams)
Aria in Ice
Cold Wind to Valhalla

Mystery
Serenade to a Cuckoo
Sweet Cream Ladies, Ltd.
Pick up the Pieces.

Romance/ Romantic Suspense
Legacy of Silence
Hot Stuff

Printed in the USA
CPSIA information can be obtained
at www.ICGtesting.com
LVHW011953020924
789879LV00030B/1182